GERALD VERNER

THE TWELVE APOSTLES

D0996207

Complete and Unabridged

LINFORD
Leicester

First published in Great Britain

First Linford Edition
published 2017

A catalogue record for this book is available
from the British Library.

ISBN 978–1–4448–3385–0

Published by
F. A. Thorpe (Publishing)
Anstey, Leicestershire

Set by Words & Graphics Ltd.
Anstey, Leicestershire
Printed and bound in Great Britain by
T. J. International Ltd., Padstow, Cornwall

This book is printed on acid-free paper

Author's Note

The story of *The Twelve Apostles* is founded on fact — or I should say that part of it which deals with the concealment of the Abbey's treasure at the time of the dissolution of the monasteries. This is a matter of history, and the particular treasure mentioned in this book actually exists and is still being sought by archaeologists who, I believe, a few years ago were within measurable distance of finding it.

The village of Monk's Ferry and its inhabitants, Felsbank Abbey, Abbotsway, and all the other places, incidents, and people described are, it is perhaps needless to state, but figments of the imagination, evolved from that queer hinterland of the mind which is an author's especial prerogative.

GERALD VERNER
November 1944.

1

The Passing of Lew Cator

The queer business of the Silver Saints and the tragic series events at Monk's Ferry began, so far as Mr. Budd was concerned, on a wet November evening in London when Lew Cator was run down by an unidentified motor vehicle and left for dead in the streaming gutter of a narrow street off the Kennington Road. When they picked him up he was unconscious, but on the way to the infirmary he recovered for a sufficient length of time to request that the stout superintendent should be sent for, and there was so much urgency in his demand that the police telephoned Scotland Yard at once.

Mr. Budd had gone home, but the message was relayed to his little house in Streatham; and when he learned who it was who wanted him, and what had happened, he agreed to come immediately. There is often a peculiar kind of camaraderie between professional thief-taker and professional thief, and the big man liked the little burglar who, according to his own queer code, always played the game. Lew had a horror of violence in any shape or form and was bitterly opposed to those members of his calling who made use of it.

'It's just a game o' wits between the p'lice an' me,' he had declared on more than one occasion. 'If I get away — that's one up to me. If I'm copped — well, it's just too bad!'

Within thirty minutes of the message reaching him, Mr. Budd was standing beside the narrow bed in which Lew Cator lay, wondering if his hurried journey had not been in vain, for the doctor made no secret of the fact that there was very little chance of Lew's recovery. He had received severe head injuries and was suffering from considerable cerebral haemorrhage. It was more than probable that he would die without regaining consciousness again.

Curious to know the reason that had prompted Lew's insistent demand for his presence, Mr. Budd decided to wait, and, balancing his enormous bulk uncomfortably on a very small and exceptionally hard chair, hoped for the best.

It was in the small hours of the morning that his patient vigil was rewarded. Quite suddenly there came a subtle change in the unconscious man's respiration. It grew louder and less regular and was accompanied by a twitching spasm of his thin body. The doctor was instantly at the bedside, alert and watchful.

'I think he's coming round,' he whispered, and the superintendent hoisted himself to his feet with a sigh of relief.

Lew Cator moved restlessly, groaned, and opened his eyes. For a moment the eyelids flickered uncertainly; and his forehead, under the bandages, puckered with pain. 'Oh, Gawd, my 'ead!' The weak voice was almost inaudible. 'It . . . it 'urts . . . like 'ell . . . '

'Keep still.' The doctor pressed a gentle hand on the wrinkled brow. 'It won't hurt so much if you don't move.'

The pain-clouded eyes stared up at him in bewilderment and alarm. ''Ere, what's this . . . ? What's 'appenin' . . . ?'

'You've been in an accident,' said Mr. Budd, bending over the bed. 'Don't you remember?'

'Accident?' The little burglar looked at him vacantly.

'You got knocked down by a car,' explained the big man. 'I'm afraid it hurt you pretty badly, Lew.'

'Oh . . . it's you . . . is it?' A spark of understanding came into the blank eyes. 'I . . . asked 'em . . . ter send for yer.' He spoke haltingly and with an obvious effort, slurring the words so that they were barely distinguishable.

'An' here I am!' said Mr. Budd cheerfully. 'What did you want me for, eh?'

'Got sump'n ter tell you . . . sump'n important . . . ' He stopped and swallowed with difficulty, his wizened face dewed with tiny beads of sweat.

'Come now, take it easy, Lew,' murmured Mr. Budd warningly. 'You 'aven't got a train to catch, you know.'

'Shan't catch no ... more trains,' whispered Lew huskily. 'I've got mine ... this time.' He paused again, recovered his breath, and went on: 'Listen ... 'e wanted me ... ter get the key ... the perisher ... '

'Who wanted you ter get what key?' asked the puzzled Mr. Budd as the dying man moistened his dry lips with the tip of his tongue.

'The Abbot's Key.' The small amount of strength that still remained was rapidly oozing away. 'The feller ... in the car wanted it ... wasn't no accident ... '

'What are you tryin' to tell me, Lew?' said Mr. Budd gravely. 'That you was deliberately run down?'

'That's it.' Lew Cator's voice was so faint now that the big man had to bend down until his ear almost touched the other's lips to catch what he said. 'I wouldn't 'ave nuthin' ter do with it ... so 'e got me ... '

A sudden convulsion shook the frail body, and the doctor leaned forward anxiously. He thought the faint spark of life had gone out, but it hadn't — quite.

'A million quid . . . ' The words came in a hoarse rattle. 'A million quid . . . the Twelve Apostles . . . ' He coughed feebly, and his hands clawed at the bed cover for a moment and then went limp.

Mr. Budd straightened up, wiping his face with his handkerchief. He did not need to wait for the doctor's verdict to know that Lew Cator was dead. 'D'you think he knew what he was talkin' about?' he asked after a pause.

'If you mean was he delirious — no,' answered the doctor gently, covering the dead man's face with the thin coverlet. 'There was intelligence in his eyes — I was watching them.'

The big man thoughtfully massaged the lowest of his many chins between a finger and thumb. 'I wonder what he was gettin' at?'

'It's clear enough, isn't it?' The doctor was tired and a little impatient, anxious to finish what he had to do and get home. 'It wasn't an accident, that's what he wanted to tell you. The man in the car ran him down on purpose.'

'Oh, yes — that's clear enough. It's all

this rigmarole about an Abbot's Key, a million quid, an' Twelve Apostles that I can't get the 'ang of.'

'Perhaps you'll discover what he meant by that when you find the man who drove the car,' suggested the doctor, yawning.

'Maybe,' said Mr. Budd doubtfully, 'an' maybe not. Maybe it isn't goin' to be so easy to find that feller.'

And, as it proved, he was right; for in spite of all the usual inquiries, no trace of the car or its unknown driver came to light. Lew Cator had been dead and buried for many weeks, and the circumstances of his death had become a vague memory in the back of Mr. Budd's mind, before the identity of his murderer was discovered — and with it, the solution of as queer and mysterious a business as any in which the stout superintendent had ever become involved.

2

The Shannons of Abbotsway

The little village of Monk's Ferry lies snugly in a fold of the Blankshire Downs within an hour's car journey of Barnford, the nearest town, and sixty miles from the great military centre of Aldershot. It is one of the few beauty spots of rural England that has escaped the spreading cancer of the ubiquitous builder, and its fields and meadows, farms and pastures, cottages and narrow-fronted shops are very much the same as they were when the eighth Henry, of dubious memory, was occupying the English throne, and the great Abbey of Felsbank stood in stately grandeur by the shallow river from which it derived its name. The river itself has long since dried up, though its course can still be traced by a winding, grass-covered depression, and of the once imposing abbey all that remains is a great heap of blackened moss-grown

8

stones, a truncated tower, and a portion of the big central arch, all slowly crumbling to the dust that has already claimed the simple and saintly men who lived and laboured within its walls.

It was said that when Henry's men, at the dissolution of the monasteries, sacked Felsbank Abbey, they had been dissatisfied with the treasures they found there and put the abbot to torture, and that ever since on certain nights his cowled figure could be seen flitting among the ruins, wringing its hands and moaning in anguish. That no one in the neighbourhood could be found who had actually witnessed this phenomenon in no way detracted from a belief in its authenticity, and there were few of the inhabitants of Monk's Ferry who would willingly linger in the vicinity of the ill-omened place after nightfall.

One of the few people who openly scoffed at the legend was Colonel Shannon. He lived in Abbotsway, the old fifteenth-century house that stood within sight of the ruins, and therefore considered himself competent to pass judgment.

'All stuff and nonsense!' he declared vehemently whenever the subject cropped up. 'I've been here for nearly five years and I've never seen or heard anything of the sort. Ghosts — rubbish!'

His wife, a woman in her late fifties whom long sojourn under hot suns had reduced to a nondescript greyness, was less sceptical, but lacked the courage to put her opinion into words; for Colonel Shannon had carried the rigid discipline of his long army career into retirement and ruled his household with military strictness.

The only one who received any latitude at all was his daughter Eileen, and he allowed her certain little indulgences — to the ill-suppressed annoyance of his son, who considered, perhaps not unreasonably, that such favouritism was unjust. He was watching her now, on this sunny spring morning, standing at the open window of his study and looking across the shaven lawn to where she was gathering spring flowers for the house.

With her slim figure, corn-coloured hair, and soft colouring, Eileen Shannon, at twenty-three, seemed to have acquired some of the beauty and grace of the daffodils she was plucking. She came leisurely back over the grass, a great sheaf of yellow blooms in her arms, and glancing up saw her father standing at the open window. 'Hello,' she called. 'Is breakfast ready?'

Colonel Shannon glanced at his wrist-watch. 'Ten minutes to go yet. It's only twenty minutes past eight.'

Everything at Abbotsway was run by the clock, and woe betide the unfortunate person, servant or otherwise, who upset the scheduled timetable by so much as a minute.

'I'll have time to put these flowers in water, then,' said Eileen. 'Is Mother down yet?'

The colonel shook his head. 'Only just come out of the bathroom,' he replied in his abrupt, clipped manner of speech. 'You were up early this morning, m'dear.'

'Yes, I didn't sleep very well.'

He saw that she looked worried. Her face was a little pale, and there were faint shadows under her eyes. 'Why, weren't you feeling well?' he asked.

'It wasn't that.' She hesitated. 'Did you — did you hear anything during the night?'

'Never hear anything,' declared her father with great satisfaction, as though it was something of which he was immensely proud. 'Sleep like a top — always have. What was it you heard?'

Again she hesitated. 'I can't very well shout to you up there,' she said after a moment. 'Besides, I must get these daffodils in water before breakfast, and I shan't have time unless I hurry. I'll tell you presently.' She waved her hand and disappeared into the house.

Colonel Shannon frowned, a little concerned about her, turned away from the window, and crossing the big book-lined room, opened the door. At sixty-five he was a tall, erect man, very spruce and immaculate, with close-cropped grey hair and a lean, tanned face. As he descended the stairs, his son came into the hall below. His shoes were white with dust, and he looked tired and rather dishevelled. His father's keen eyes noted his appearance and an expression of displeasure crossed his stern face.

'Michael!' he called sharply, and Michael Shannon stopped with his hand on the handle of the dining-room door and looked up.

'Good morning, Father,' he said uneasily.

'Where have you been?' The colonel ran quickly down the rest of the stairs and came to his side.

'I — I've been for a walk,' answered Michael a little sullenly. 'It was a lovely morning, and I thought — '

'Hm!' His father looked him swiftly up and down. His dark hair was ruffled, and there was a smear of dirt across one sallow cheek, and a long cut on his chin from which the blood had trickled onto his creased collar. 'Looks more as if you've been in a fight than out for a walk. How did you get yourself in that disgusting state?'

Michael flushed, and his eyes evaded his father's penetrating gaze. 'I . . . I slipped climbing over the stile by Long Meadow,' he muttered, but his voice lacked conviction.

'Better go and clean yourself up,' said the colonel brusquely. 'Can't come to breakfast like that. Better be quick too,' he added as he caught sight of the big grandfather clock near the hall door. 'You've only got three minutes.'

Without a word, Michael turned and began to hurry up the stairs, limping a little as he did so.

'Don't forget to shave,' the colonel called after him, and he went into the dining-room with a slightly ruffled temper.

Mrs. Shannon had not yet put in an appearance, but Eileen was putting the finishing touches to a big cut-glass vase of daffodils that stood in the centre of the long refectory table, while Bream, the elderly butler, was arranging some silver dishes on the carved oak sideboard.

'Was that Mickey you were speaking to?' asked Eileen, looking up as her father came in.

'Yes,' he answered shortly, and he went over to the sideboard to inspect the breakfast dishes, so that he failed to see the worried frown come to his daughter's

14

face. 'Hm,' he said, lifting each cover and glancing at the contents, 'kidneys and bacon, poached eggs, kedgeree — excellent!' He glanced at his watch. 'Bring in the coffee and toast, Bream.'

'Very good, sir.' The butler went over to the door, but stood aside as it opened and Mrs. Shannon came quickly in.

'I'm not late, am I?' she asked a little apprehensively as she took her place at the foot of the table.

'Punctual to the minute, Alice,' said the colonel approvingly. 'What would you like?' He ran through the contents of the dishes.

'Oh, I don't know.' Mrs. Shannon dabbed at her thin nose with a tiny wisp of a handkerchief and looked at the grapefruit in front of her. 'Just grapefruit and a slice of toast, I think.'

The colonel frowned. 'You can't go until lunch-time on *that*,' he said — he was a great believer in the health value of food. 'Have some eggs?'

'Well, perhaps I'll have just one,' said Mrs. Shannon uncertainly. 'Really, I'm not very hungry.'

'You ought to be hungry.' Colonel Shannon sat down and opened his napkin. 'Not hungry . . . can't be well.'

'I'm perfectly well,' said Mrs. Shannon, who was one of those people who disliked large quantities of food first thing in the morning, a fact which no amount of reiteration had ever been able to make the colonel understand. 'I never did care very much for breakfast. You know that, James.'

'Good for you,' said her husband with his mouth full of grapefruit. 'Sound foundation to start the day.'

Bream came in with the coffee and toast and set the silver tray down in front of his mistress. 'Thank you, Bream,' she said, and then as he withdrew: 'Where's Michael?'

'I sent him upstairs to clean up.' The colonel touched his lips with his napkin, got up and went over to the sideboard. 'Young beggar went out for a walk early and fell over a stile or something. Came back in a shocking mess. Hadn't even troubled to shave, either.' He helped himself liberally to kidneys and bacon and carried his plate to the table. 'Ready for your eggs, Alice?'

'Thank you, James.' Mrs. Shannon was busy pouring out the coffee. 'Only one, please.'

'What will you have, Eileen?'

But she was staring at her plate, her thoughts apparently miles away, and he had to repeat the question before she heard him. 'I — I don't think I want anything, thank you, Father,' she said in a low voice.

'Begad, what's the matter with all of you?' demanded the colonel tartly.

'I've got a headache,' answered Eileen.

Her mother gave her an anxious glance. 'Have you, dear? You'd better take some aspirin.'

'Oh, I remember. Said you didn't sleep very well,' said the colonel, deftly slicing a poached egg out of the dish onto a hot plate. 'Asked me if I'd heard anything during the night. What disturbed you?'

Before she could answer him, the door opened and Michael came in. He had washed and shaved and changed his clothes, but he looked tired and rather wan. Eileen gave him a searching, questioning look as he sat down at the table opposite her.

'You look a bit under the weather, me lad,' remarked the colonel, eyeing his son critically as he handed his wife her egg. 'Something disturb you in the night too, eh?'

Michael gave a start and nearly dropped the spoon he had picked up. 'Disturb me?' he repeated uneasily. 'No, why?' He looked quickly round the table, met his sister's eyes, and hurriedly avoided them.

'Eileen says she heard something and couldn't sleep,' said the colonel. 'What was it, m'dear?'

'I don't quite know,' replied his daughter hesitantly. 'It — it sounded like a scream.'

'You must have been dreaming,' remarked the colonel, busy with his kidneys and bacon.

Eileen shook her head. 'No, I wasn't dreaming,' she declared with conviction. 'I'd been asleep, and then I suddenly woke up with the noise in my ears. It came from outside the house — a

18

horrible scream, like someone in great pain. It terrified me. It was beastly!' She shivered at the recollection.

'Night bird,' said the colonel practically, 'or nightmare! What time was it?'

'Half-past one. I put on the light at once and looked at the clock by my bed. I'm sure it was *someone* who screamed. It wasn't a nightmare, and it didn't sound like any night bird I've ever heard.'

'They make queer noises sometimes,' said the colonel. 'Remember the row they used to kick up in India, Alice? Like a regiment of howling dervishes. Couldn't have been anybody screaming round here. Nearest house is half a mile away, and no one 'ud be out at that hour.'

'It seemed to come from the ruins of the old abbey,' said Eileen. She heard her mother's sharp intake of breath.

The colonel snorted. 'Not suggesting it was the abbot, are you?' he grunted, helping himself to a slice of toast and spreading it carefully with butter.

'I'm not suggesting anything,' said Eileen quietly. 'I'm only telling you what I heard.' She was only telling *part* of what she had heard during the night, but of this he was, happily, unaware.

'What you heard, if you didn't dream it, m'dear,' said the colonel, reaching for the marmalade, 'was either a night bird or an animal. I can't understand — What is it, Bream?'

The elderly butler had entered quietly, and was standing deferentially by the door. 'If you please, sir,' he said apologetically, 'the gardener would like to speak to you.'

'Can't see him now,' snapped the colonel irritably. 'I'm in the middle of breakfast.'

'I'm sorry, sir.' Bream was respectful but firm. 'But the matter is rather urgent. I think it would be advisable if you could make it convenient to see him at once, sir.'

'Eh, what!' Colonel Shannon was so astonished at the temerity of this suggestion that he could scarcely speak. 'What the devil do you mean, Bream? I won't — '

'Something very serious has occurred, sir,' interrupted the butler. 'Very serious indeed.'

'Serious?' barked his master, and the

old man nodded. 'Well, what is it? Tell me and I'll see if it's serious enough to interrupt my breakfast.'

The butler hesitated, glancing quickly from one to the other, his lined face troubled and paler than usual.

'Go on, man!' exclaimed the colonel impatiently. 'What's the matter?'

'The gardener . . . ' he began huskily, and cleared his throat. 'The gardener has just found the dead body of a man in the abbey ruins, sir.'

'What's that?' The colonel's startled exclamation drowned the stifled cry that Eileen uttered. 'A dead man in the ruins? What sort of a man? A tramp?'

'No, sir,' answered Bream. 'A gentleman who's been staying at The Monk's Head in the village, sir.'

'Good God!' said Colonel Shannon, gaping in astonishment. 'How did he die?'

'The gardener says he was stabbed, sir,' replied the butler gravely.

'That was the scream I heard,' whispered Eileen. Her face was the colour of chalk.

3

The Man Who was Killed

The assistant commissioner laid the telephone back on its rack, stared thoughtfully for a minute at the notes he had scribbled on the pad in front of him, and then pressed a button at his elbow. 'See if you can find Superintendent Budd,' he said to the uniformed messenger who answered his summons. 'If he's in his office, ask him to come and see me at once.'

When the messenger had gone, he lay back in his chair looking at the dingy ceiling and carefully smoothing the back of his immaculate grey head with the palm of his right hand. He was thus engaged when there came a tap on the door, and Mr. Budd walked ponderously into the office.

'Good morning, Superintendent,' greeted Colonel Blair. 'Sit down, will you? I've got a job for you.'

Mr. Budd did so, evoking a protesting

22

crack from the chair, which had not been designed to carry people of his bulk.

'Yes, sir?' he murmured.

'I've an idea that it may turn out to be quite a big job,' went on the assistant commissioner, leaning forward and straightening the papers on his blotting-pad. 'There's been a murder at a little place called Monk's Ferry, near Aldershot, and the chief constable of Blankshire has asked for the assistance of the Yard. The body of a man was found in the ruins of an old abbey at eight-fifteen this morning, by a gardener employed at a house called Abbotsway. The house is close to the ruins, and the gardener had taken a barrow to collect stones for a rockery he was building when he made the discovery. The man had been stabbed in the left side, and the gardener recognized him at once as a gentleman who had been staying at the local inn — a Mr. Lloyd Gibbs.'

Mr. Budd, who had been listening with his eyes almost completely closed, suddenly jerked them open to their widest extent. 'Lloyd Gibbs!' he exclaimed in astonishment.

Colonel Blair's rather stern mouth twitched slightly at the corners. 'I thought that would surprise you. It's rare for a newspaper man to get murdered, and when he happens to be the principal crime reporter for a paper like the *Post-Courier*, it looks to me as if there might be something very big attached to it.'

Mr. Budd nodded slowly. He had recovered from his momentary surprise, and was once again his stolid, lethargic self. 'I think maybe you're right, sir,' he remarked thoughtfully. 'I s'pose it was because of the position of the dead man that the local authorities was so quick in callin' us in?'

'I think so,' agreed the assistant commissioner. 'They're probably a little scared of what the *Post-Courier* would have to say if they tried to clear this up off their own bat and failed. It's a very good thing, because now you'll be in at the start before any clues there may be have got cold.'

'Why was this poor feller Gibbs stayin' at what's-the-place — Monk's Ferry? Was he coverin' somethin' for his paper?'

Colonel Blair shook his neat head. 'That I can't tell you. It's up to you to find out. They'll know at the *Post-Courier* office, of course. I should think it was more than likely, and that he found out something that someone didn't want found out. However, I can't tell you anything more than I have. Superintendent Boyder of the Blankshire Police is in charge of the case, and he'll give you all the details that are known.'

'I'll get started right away, sir,' said Mr. Budd, hoisting himself with difficulty out of the chair and moving heavily over to the door.

'Good luck,' said Colonel Blair. Pulling a bulky folder forward on his desk, he became immersed in its contents as the big man left the office.

Dipping a finger and thumb into his waistcoat pocket, Mr. Budd pulled out a thin black cigar and sniffed at it appreciatively as he made his way back to his own cheerless little room. His heavy lids drooped over his eyes, and his face wore an expression of such unutterable boredom that anyone who knew him well would have known that his brain was busy and alert.

Sergeant Leek, his lean form hunched uncomfortably on a hard chair, was chewing the end of a pencil and frowning ferociously at a paper balanced on his bony knee, when his superior entered the office.

'Pickin' losers again?' grunted Mr. Budd disparagingly, lumbering over to his desk and wedging himself in his chair. 'The time you waste over 'orses that never win is enough ter make Sir Robert Peel turn in 'is grave.'

Leek looked up gloomily. 'I've given up 'orses. I've gone ter the dogs.'

'You never spoke a truer word in yer life,' said Mr. Budd unkindly. He struck a match, lit his cigar, and blew out a cloud of evil-smelling smoke with great satisfaction.

'I mean the grey'ounds,' said the sergeant in painful explanation. 'A feller was tellin' me yesterday that you can make a lot o' money if you back the right trap.'

'Forget it,' snapped Mr. Budd, 'an' concentrate for a change on earnin' yer salary. We've got a job to do.' He gave a brief resumé of his interview with the assistant commissioner. 'I'm goin' along to see the news editor of the *Post-Courier*,' he concluded, rising to his feet and reaching for his hat. 'You can do as you like for the next hour; but I shall want you to be ready then to start for this place, Monk's Ferry. We may 'ave to stay there for a bit, so you'd better pack a bag. An' don't go bringin' any grey'ounds,' he added severely as he went out.

His dingy little car, which his colleagues watched daily in the hopeful expectancy of seeing fall to pieces, carried him to Fleet Street, and the imposing offices of the *Post-Courier*. The taciturn news editor, a disillusioned man with a conviction that the milk of human kindness was a myth, saw him at once. But the interview did nothing to clear up the reason for Lloyd Gibbs's death. He had not been working for the *Post-Courier* when he had gone to stay at Monk's Ferry. He had been on a fortnight's holiday which he had asked for and been granted, because his doctor had ordered him a rest and a change. The news editor could suggest no one who might have had a sufficient grudge against him to have wished to kill him, though he admitted that there were times when he had had murderous inclinations himself.

Gibbs had been a brilliant reporter with that passion for wanting to know, which is the hallmark of the born newspaper man, but he had also possessed a queer secretive strain. He liked to keep what he learned to himself until he had all the details perfect — a characteristic that the people with, and for whom, he worked, found particularly exasperating. Mr. Budd, who had the same peculiarity, could both understand and sympathize.

He left the *Post-Courier* offices with the feeling that if he had not altogether wasted his time, he had learned nothing that was helpful. The motive for the murder of Lloyd Gibbs must lie further back in his past and, quite possibly, had nothing to do with his professional activities at all. And yet ... The superintendent was very thoughtful as he drove back to Scotland Yard.

He found Sergeant Leek gloomily waiting for him beside a battered old Gladstone bag. Collecting his own suit-case, which he always kept ready-packed in his office in case of just such an emergency as this, he went back with the lugubrious sergeant to his car and set off in that ancient machine for Monk's Ferry.

They reached the little village just after one o'clock and pulled up, after inquiring the way, in front of the local police station, which consisted of a pretty half-timbered cottage standing in a tiny garden full of spring flowers.

'Nice little place,' murmured Mr. Budd, eyeing it appreciatively as he clambered laboriously out of his car. 'These rural fellers 'ave all the luck.'

A thick-set man with a round, ruddy face and a grizzled moustache appeared in the doorway as he opened the gate and came halfway down the path to meet him. 'Superintendent Budd?' he inquired, and when Mr. Budd nodded: 'I'm Superintendent Boyder. My headquarters are over at

Barnford, but I thought you'd come here first, so I waited for you.'

'Glad to meet you,' said Mr. Budd as they shook hands. 'This is Sergeant Leek.' He introduced the melancholy sergeant, who was hovering uncertainly behind him.

'Shall we go inside?' suggested Boyder. 'I expect you'll be thinking it's a bit primitive, but it suits these parts. There's very little crime round 'ere as a rule; vagrancy an' one or two poultry thefts, that's all. Anything bigger we 'andle at Barnford.'

He led the way inside the cottage while he was speaking. It was a very old place with low ceilings and heavy oak beams. The small parlour was furnished partly as a sitting-room and partly as an office, with a faded green baize-covered board over a plain table on which had been pinned up various official notices. An ancient wall-telephone occupied a space beside this, and there were two horsehair-covered armchairs and a sofa. Mr. Budd learned that this very rural police station was in the sole charge of a constable named Fowler, who was a bachelor and lived on the premises.

'Now,' said the big man when they were seated, 'let's hear all about this business.'

Superintendent Boyder produced a bulky black notebook from an inside pocket, cleared his throat, and began a recital of the details relating to the discovery of the body. Mr. Budd, leaning back in his chair with his eyes closed and his hands clasped loosely over his capacious stomach, listened attentively, though as far as outward appearances went he might have been enjoying a comfortable forty winks.

The facts which the local man had so far managed to collect were meagre. The doctor's evidence suggested that the crime had been committed in the very early hours of the morning — sometime between one and two o'clock. This was substantiated by Colonel Shannon's daughter, who had been awakened by a scream at half-past one which, she said, had come from the direction of the abbey ruins.

'Who's Colonel Shannon?' murmured Mr. Budd without opening his eyes.

'He bought the house about four years ago,' Boyder explained. 'It was put up for sale, lock, stock an' barrel, after the previous owner, Everitt Marie, was arrested an' sent to prison for fraud. I expect you remember the case?'

Mr. Budd grunted. He remembered the case very well. ''E was a financier an' did some fiddlin' with shares. There was a lot of money involved, an' he got four years. He died in the prison infirmary last October.'

'That's right,' Boyder said, nodding in agreement with this brief biography. 'Well, 'e used to live at this place Abbotsway. Colonel Shannon, when he retired from some sort o' government post in India, was looking for a house an' bought it.'

'An' his daughter heard a scream in the middle of the night,' said Mr. Budd, 'which was prob'ly Gibbs's death cry. Hm, I've got all that. Well, what else?'

'That's about all,' confessed the local superintendent disappointedly. 'No weapon was found, or anything on the scene of the crime that you could call even the shadow of a clue.'

Mr. Budd yawned wearily and opened his eyes. Fumbling in his waistcoat pocket, he produced one of his inevitable black cigars, stuck it between his teeth, and lit it. 'I'm not offerin' you one o' these,' he said, 'because the last feller I gave one to threatened to take legal proceedings.' He blew out a great cloud of foul smoke. 'This feller, Gibbs,' he went on slowly, 'was stayin' at the local pub, wasn't he?'

'Yes,' replied Boyder, waving away the smoke that was drifting round him and coughing slightly. 'He'd been there for just on nine days.'

'Did you search 'is room?'

Boyder nodded. 'There was nothing helpful.'

'The thing that strikes me as bein' queer,' murmured Mr. Budd, 'is why he was prowlin' around those ruins in the middle o' the night.' He looked at his watch. 'What sort o' beer do they serve at this pub where Gibbs was stayin'?'

'Pretty good,' said Boyder.

The superintendent hoisted himself ponderously to his feet. 'Then we may as well go along an' sample it. There's nothin' like a good drop o' beer ter give yer ideas, an' it looks ter me as though we're goin' ter need a lot before we get to the bottom o' this business.'

'Beer or ideas?' asked Boyder with a twinkle in his eyes.

'Both,' answered Mr. Budd.

4

The Woman Who was Afraid

The Monk's Head was a pleasant-looking inn standing in a sort of bay at the end of the narrow high street. Like the majority of the older buildings in the village, it was half-timbered, with leaded windows and a gabled roof of mellowed tiles. Although certain restorations had been necessary in the passing of time, these had been carried out carefully and in keeping with the architecture of the period.

Mr. Jephcott, the round-faced, genial landlord, could trace his pedigree back almost to the date of the original building, and was immensely proud of the fact. There had, he was fond of boasting, always been a Jephcott at The Monk's Head, and his rapidly growing family suggested that there always would be.

He was leaning on the counter in the long raftered bar, talking to a hatless young man with unruly red hair in a well-worn suit of tweed, when Mr. Budd, Superintendent Boyder, and the melancholy Leek came in.

There were not many other people in the place. Mr. Budd noted the few who were there in one sweeping, apparently sleepy-eyed glance as he followed Boyder over to the bar. Three men who looked like farmers were lounging at the bar drinking beer. An elderly man was sitting at a table in one of the windows reading a newspaper, an empty sherry glass in front of him; and in a corner by herself was a smartly dressed, attractive woman smoking a cigarette and sipping a whisky and ginger ale.

Mr. Jephcott broke off his low-voiced conversation with the young man in Harris tweed and came to see what they wanted. His late companion turned round, a tankard in his hand, and, catching sight of Mr. Budd, stopped with it halfway to his lips. A broad grin spread across his freckled face and he walked over to join them.

'Well, well,' he greeted pleasantly. 'If it

isn't the great detective himself — or should I have said enormous?'

Mr. Budd eyed him resentfully. 'I don't want any of your sauce, Walton,' he grunted. 'How did you get 'ere?'

'On a motorbike,' said Peter Walton cheerfully. He emptied his tankard and set it down on the counter. 'So they've put you in charge of this business, have they? Hm, that's good.'

'Maybe you won't find it so good,' growled Mr. Budd.

'Now you're not going to be awkward, are you? I'm covering this murder for the *Post-Courier*, and I'll probably be very useful to you. Buy me a beer and let's get together.'

'I'll buy you nuthin',' said Mr. Budd ungraciously, 'an' it's no good you pesterin' me for information because you won't get any.'

Peter looked at him quizzically. He had worked with this bovine-looking, sleepy-eyed man on several cases before, and he knew that his bark was a great deal worse than his bite. 'Supposing the boot is on the other foot,' he suggested gently.

'Supposing *I* might be able to give *you* a little information?'

'I've heard that one before,' said Mr. Budd sceptically. 'What sort of information?'

Peter winked. 'That's telling. If you're willing to pool everything — well, that might be a different matter.'

Mr. Budd hesitated. Peter Walton was a skilful newspaper man with a flair for nosing out facts that was uncanny. He was not quite as brilliant as Lloyd Gibbs had been, and for this reason had mostly been assigned to the less-important crime cases by the *Post-Courier*; but he ran him a very close second, and there was little doubt that he would take his place. If this turned out to be the big job that it appeared to be, Peter's assistance might prove invaluable, for he had been intimate with the dead man.

'I'll tell you what I'll do,' said Mr. Budd with great generosity. 'I'll exchange ideas with you over this business, provided that you promise you won't print anythin' in that rag o' yours without my permission.'

'Sell my birthright for a mess of

pottage, eh?' Peter grinned. 'It's a deal — on one condition.'

'What?'

'That I get an exclusive story for the *Courier* in the end.'

Mr. Budd agreed. 'Now, what's this information you've got?' he asked.

'Can't tell you now,' said Peter with a quick glance at the others. 'It 'ud take too long. We'll have a chat later.'

Mr. Budd introduced him to Boyder, and the local man called for another pint of beer — he had already ordered two for himself and the stout man. The melancholy Leek never drank anything but lime juice and soda, which was why, Mr. Budd always asserted, he looked so sour.

'I've been expecting someone from the *Post-Courier*,' said Boyder, 'to identify the dead man.'

'That's me,' said Peter. 'I was on my way to find you when I saw this place and thought I'd just drop in for a quick one. Where have you taken the body?'

'To the mortuary at Barnford,' answered the local superintendent.

'I'd like to come with you when you

make the identification,' murmured Mr. Budd, staring sleepily at the contents of his tankard. 'But there's one or two things I want ter do here first. I want to 'ave a look at the room Gibbs occupied, an' 'ave a little chat to the landlord. An' I'd also like to see these ruins an' meet this gal who 'eard the scream.' He swallowed the remainder of his beer. 'We'll just 'ave another,' he said, 'an' then we'll get busy.'

Mr. Jephcott refilled the tankards, and on Mr. Budd's invitation drew one for himself. The three men who looked like farmers had gone, and the bar was empty except for themselves, the elderly man, who was still deep in his newspaper, and the woman in the corner. Mr. Budd had been covertly watching her for some time. There was something about her that set a tiny cell in his brain quivering, but the elusive memory only stirred sluggishly and refused to come to life. He was certain all the same that sometime, somewhere, he had seen her before. He leaned across the bar and put a question to the landlord, but Mr. Jephcott shook his bald head.

'I've never seen the lady before, sir,' he replied. 'She's a stranger in these parts.'

Peter Walton, who had heard the murmured question, grinned wickedly. 'Now, now,' he said severely, 'no philandering. Keep your mind on your job.'

Mr. Budd ignored him and continued to talk to the landlord. 'This feller, Gibbs,' he said conversationally, 'had been staying with you for some time, hadn't he?'

'Matter of nine days,' answered Mr. Jephcott. 'He booked the room for a fortnight when he came. Terrible thing to have 'appened. It don't really seem possible . . .'

'How did he spend his time? Did he have any visitors while he was 'ere?'

'No, sir.' The landlord took a pull at his tankard. 'No one ever came to see him, an' he spent most of his time out. Very interested in 'istory, he was, an' these parts is, as you might say, steeped in it. Writin' a book, he said he was.'

'Hm, writin' a book, was he?' murmured Mr. Budd. 'What time did he usually come in at night?'

'At all hours. He asked me for a key to the side door when he first came. Said he suffered from insomnia, and the only thing that 'ud make him sleep was a long walk after supper. He used to say good night to me on the way out, an' I wouldn't see 'im again until he came down in the mornin'. I don't rightly know what time he came in. He was always very quiet.'

'I'd like to have a look at his room,' said Mr. Budd. 'An' while we're on the subject of rooms, d'you think you could put us up fer a night or two?'

The landlord thought he could manage one room. The only other vacant one he had already agreed to let Peter Walton have.

'Sergeant Leek can stay with Fowler,' put in Boyder, coming to the rescue. 'He's got a spare room an' he'll be glad of the company.'

'Well, that's that, then,' said Mr. Budd. 'Now let's 'ave a look at Gibbs's room.'

Boyder had the key and, at Mr. Jephcott's suggestion, agreed to take them up. As they left the bar, Mr. Budd saw the woman in the corner get up and brush down her skirt. Their eyes met, and again that elusive memory bothered him. But he could not place her.

Peter caught his arm as they went up the narrow staircase. 'I say, that stuff about insomnia was all bunk. Gibbs used to boast that nothing could wake him and that he could sleep anywhere.'

Mr. Budd grunted. 'I guessed that. But it was a very good excuse for his havin' a key an' bein' out till all hours. The thing is, why did he want to?'

They had reached the head of the stairs which opened on to a narrow passage that ran from back to front of the building. There were four doors opening from this, two on either side. In front of the second door on the left, Boyder stopped, pulled the key from his pocket, and twisted it in the lock.

The room which they presently entered was pleasant and smelt jointly of lavender and tobacco smoke. The furniture was old and solid, and the wide casement window was hung with faded chintz. The bed had not been slept in, but there was evidence of Gibbs's occupancy in the litter of pipes, books, magazines, and papers which lay on a table in the window, and a suit that hung over the back of a chair near the fireplace.

Mr. Budd stood near the door and sleepily took stock of the place. Then he went ponderously over to the table and examined the contents. The books were mostly novels, with the exception of one, which was a guide to Blankshire. There was a slip of paper between the pages marking that portion which dealt with Monk's Ferry and the surrounding district. There was nothing else of interest, and Mr. Budd turned his attention to the rest of the room.

A large suitcase at the foot of the bed contained shirts, underclothes, and socks, some handkerchiefs, and a couple of ties, but there was nothing to suggest why Lloyd Gibbs had walked the countryside at night or the reason for his death. Nor was there anything in the room that was at all helpful, although Mr. Budd subjected it to a rigorous search.

'He had his wallet on him, I s'pose,' he

remarked wearily when he had finished. 'He must 'a done, or you wouldn't have known that he was connected with the *Post-Courier*.'

'There was nothing in it except some money in notes and a few cards,' said Superintendent Boyder. 'It was the cards that had the *Post-Courier*'s address on 'em. Have you finished here?'

'Yes.' Mr. Budd suppressed a yawn. 'I'll leave my bag 'ere and then we'll get along an' inspect these ruins.'

The woman in the corner had gone when they got back to the bar, and so had the elderly man with the newspaper. Mr. Budd left his bag with the landlord, and when they had succeeded in squeezing themselves into his dilapidated car, they set off for the abbey ruins.

They were a good mile from The Monk's Head, and the road that led to them was none too good. The car, its ancient springs squeaking loudly in protest, bumped and rattled over the uneven surface, and Mr. Budd drew up near the pile of black-grey stones with a sigh of relief. Easing himself with difficulty from behind the wheel, he clambered heavily down and surveyed the ruins without enthusiasm.

'Queer sort o' place ter come at half-past one in the mornin',' he remarked. 'Unless 'e wanted ter meet someone in private. Then it 'ud be a good spot ter choose, I should think. Where exactly was the body found?'

Boyder led the way among the great piles of stones and past a gaunt and broken arch. The grass and weeds grew thickly, but beneath them Mr. Budd could feel the flagstones with which the abbey had been paved. Opposite the truncated tower was a hint of the original cloisters, and here Boyder stopped and pointed to a reddish stain on the grass and moss. 'There,' he announced briefly.

Mr. Budd peered down at the sinister mark and gently rubbed his fleshy chin. 'There's no trace of a struggle,' he murmured. 'This grass here 'ud show signs if there had been. Looks as if he was taken by surprise. What'd the doctor say? Did he die at once?'

'Instantly, according to the doctor. The

knife penetrated the left side and pierced the heart.'

'Hm, interestin' an' peculiar,' said Mr. Budd. 'I must have a word with that feller.'

He stood for a minute letting his eyes rove lazily round, and then began to peer about among the grass and stones in the immediate neighbourhood.

'I've already searched the place pretty thoroughly,' said Boyder, but Mr. Budd apparently did not hear him, for he continued to hunt about without taking any notice. At last he appeared to have satisfied himself that there was nothing to be found, for he straightened up with a grunt and mopped his perspiring face.

'Hm, well,' he remarked, breathing a little heavily from his exertion. 'There's nuthin' more to be done here. Let's go an' see the gal who heard the scream.'

They left the ruins, crossed the grass-covered depression that had once been the bed of the River Pel, and presently came to the thick yew hedge that surrounded the grounds of Abbotsway. There was a gate in this, which Boyder opened, and they walked up the winding drive that led to the house.

Bream opened the big iron-studded oak door in answer to the local man's knock, and, when he learned the reason for their visit, ushered them into the hall and disappeared through a door on the left. After a short interval he reappeared, accompanied by Colonel Shannon.

'I understand you want to see my daughter again,' he said stiffly. 'I'd rather not disturb her unless it's necessary. She's lying down. Greatly upset over this business.'

'I should like just a word with her, sir,' murmured Mr. Budd apologetically. 'It's very natural she should be upset, but I won't keep her more than a minute.'

'She can't tell you any more than she did this morning,' broke in the colonel. 'Surely — '

'I didn't see her this mornin',' interrupted Mr. Budd gently. 'I'm afraid I'll have to insist on seein' her, sir, if you please.'

Colonel Shannon quite obviously did *not* please. He glared at Mr. Budd with a look that had caused many a man in his brigade to shake in his shoes, but which had no effect at all on the sleepy-eyed man before him. Then he turned abruptly to the waiting Bream. 'Ask Miss Eileen to come down,' he ordered brusquely.

The old man inclined his head and went up the massive staircase. In a few minutes he returned. 'Miss Eileen will be down in a moment, sir,' he said, and his master dismissed him with a nod and a gesture.

She came almost at once. She looked very pale and ill, and rested her hand on the carved oak banister as she slowly descended the stairs, as if to steady herself.

'Sorry to disturb you, m'dear,' said Colonel Shannon in a slightly softer tone. 'This man is a detective from Scotland Yard and insists on seeing you.'

The watchful Mr. Budd saw an expression come into her eyes at the word 'detective' that he had often seen before in others and recognized instantly. It was sheer naked terror! This woman was afraid — desperately afraid — and of him.

And the only explanation for such a fear was that she was terrified lest he should discover something that she was most anxious to conceal.

5

What Peter Knew

It was gone in a moment, that fleeting expression of terror, and was replaced by a wary look, but he knew that he had not been mistaken. This woman knew something, something that she had not divulged. The mere sound of a scream in the night, even though it proved to have heralded the violent death of a stranger, would not have reduced her to her present state of fear.

'I'm sorry to bother you, miss,' said Mr. Budd gently, 'but I've got my job ter do, an' this is part of it. I won't keep you longer than I can help.'

'Thank you. I'm not feeling very well,' she murmured faintly.

'I expect this thing 'appening on your doorstep, as you might say, has given you a bit of a shock.' Mr. Budd nodded understandingly. 'Very natural. Maybe you'd like ter sit down while I ask you a few questions?'

There was a chair by the newel post of the staircase, and she sank onto it, clasping her hands in her lap.

'Now then, miss,' went on Mr. Budd in his most avuncular manner, 'p'r'aps you'll just tell me what you 'eard durin' the night.'

She told him, and it sounded as though she were repeating a lesson she had learned by heart.

'I see,' murmured the superintendent when she came to the end of her short recital. 'You heard this scream an' it woke you up. You put on the light an' looked at the clock an' saw that it was half-past one. What did you do then?'

'I — I didn't do anything.'

'You just lay down an' went to sleep again, is that right, miss?'

'I — I didn't go to sleep again.' She had kept her eyes fixed on the hands in her lap all the time, and so had Mr. Budd, for long experience had taught him that it was sometimes possible to read more from a person's hands than from their face, and Eileen Shannon's hands betrayed her nervousness. 'I tried to, but I couldn't.'

'Whereabouts is your room, miss?' he asked. 'In the front or the back of the house?'

'In — the front.' Her fingers, which had been twisting and twining, were suddenly still.

'In the front?' repeated Mr. Budd musingly. 'That'd be facin' the ruins, wouldn't it, miss?'

'Yes.' He could scarcely hear the low-voiced answer.

'Can you see them from your winder?'

'Yes.' She hesitated for several seconds before she admitted the fact.

'Now let me see.' Mr. Budd rubbed his massive chin thoughtfully. 'There'd be a moon last night, wouldn't there? Pretty nearly a full moon?'

'Yes, there was,' put in Superintendent Boyder. 'It was a very bright night.'

'I thought so,' said Mr. Budd, nodding slowly. 'Now, miss, when you 'eard this scream, which sounded to you as if it came from outside in the direction of the ruins, surely you looked out the winder to see if you could see anything?'

Eileen raised her head for the first time, and there was no mistaking her agitation. 'No,' she said thinly. 'No, I didn't.'

Mr. Budd pursed his lips, and his sleepy eyes looked at her steadily through narrowed slits. 'Are you sure o' that, miss?' he asked, but before she could reply Colonel Shannon broke in testily.

'If my daughter says she didn't, she didn't,' he snapped. 'I don't like your insinuation, sir!'

'I wasn't insinuatin' anythin',' murmured Mr. Budd softly. 'I was just tryin' ter help Miss Shannon's memory. Very often people ferget things, an' a little reminder brings it back to 'em. It 'ud have been a very natural action, seein' there was a moon, ter look out the winder an' try an' see what had caused that scream. It's a thing almost anybody 'ud have done. If Miss Shannon says she didn't — well, there it is.' He looked at her, but she had dropped her eyes to her lap again and remained silent. 'I don't think I need keep you any longer, miss,' he said, and sighed wearily. 'It's a pity you didn't look out that winder. You might have seen somethin'.'

She got up quickly, glanced from one to the other, and turning, ran up the stairs. She was halfway up when Mr. Budd called after her. 'Oh, there's just one other thin', miss.'

She stopped and looked back over her shoulder.

'You didn't know this feller who was killed — Lloyd Gibbs, did you, miss?'

'No,' she replied, and hurried quickly round the bend of the stairway.

'What did you mean by that?' demanded Colonel Shannon, frowning angrily. 'Why should my daughter know this man?'

'There's no reason why she should, an' there's no reason why she shouldn't,' said Mr. Budd blandly. 'He'd been stayin' here fer several days, an' she might have met him in the village. Well, sir, I won't trouble you any more fer the time bein'. Maybe I could just have a word with your gardener?'

Colonel Shannon, on the point of an explosion, thought better of it, stalked over to a bell-rope and gave it an angry tug. 'Bream will take you to him,' he said icily. 'Good afternoon.' He went into the room from which he had emerged on their arrival, almost banging the door behind him.

'You've upset the old boy,' said Peter with a chuckle. 'He's as mad as an angry bull.'

'I'm goin' ter lose a lot o' sleep,' murmured Mr. Budd, yawning, 'an' he's not so much mad as worried.'

'Worried?' repeated Superintendent Boyder. 'Why — you don't think . . . ?'

'I do every now an' again,' interrupted the stout man. 'An' what I'm thinkin' at the moment is why that woman lied.'

Bream appeared and silenced the question that was burning on the tip of Peter's tongue. 'Colonel Shannon wants you ter take us to the gardener,' said Mr. Budd.

The butler bowed slightly. 'Come this way, please,' he said, and as they followed him out the front door, Mr. Budd was irresistibly reminded of a dignified shop-walker in a large store.

They found the gardener working at

the rockery that had been the cause of his making his gruesome discovery. He was a smallish man with a wizened, weather-beaten face, and the gnarled hands which seem peculiar to gardeners. He was quite willing to break off from his work and discuss an experience that would forever remain a milestone in his uneventful life.

'Yer could 'ave knocked me down with a feather,' he declared unoriginally, 'when I found 'im lyin' there starin' up at the sky with 'is clothes all over blood. I couldn't believe I wasn't seein' thin's fer a bit. At first I thought 'e must 'ave met with a h'accident — bin climbin' up the ruins an' fallen — an' then when I 'ad a closer look an' saw the slit in 'is coat — well, blimey! It sort o' took me breath away.'

'I'm sure it did,' said Mr. Budd, and he proceeded to ask several questions, from which he elicited very little more than he already knew. Mr. Adams — for such was the gardener's name — was voluble but not very helpful. He had recognized the dead man at once because he had seen him several times in the village and had once had a drink with him at The Monk's Head. He had seemed a nice sort of gentleman — very affable and free-handed. He had never seen him in the vicinity of the ruins before, but it wasn't very likely he would. He spent most of his time working in the garden of Abbotsway, and, as they could see for themselves, the high yew hedge shut out all sight of the ruins. When he finished his work he usually went down to the village, had a drink or two, and then went home to his supper and bed. He lived in a small cottage about a mile away and travelled back and forth on a bicycle.

They left the gardener, and, returning to the car, drove to Barnford, which was a fair-sized market town. The mortuary was an ugly building of very new red brick, and here Peter Walton made a formal identification of the body. Mr. Budd conducted a searching examination of the dead man's clothing and the contents of the pockets, which yielded nothing that could be twisted into the remotest semblance of a clue, then paid a visit to the police surgeon. From him, he learned that the wound must have been instantly fatal; that it had been made by a very thin-bladed knife which had severed the aortic artery, and that death had taken place between one and two o'clock in the morning.

'Which doesn't tell us anythin' we didn't know before,' grunted Mr. Budd gloomily. 'It looks ter me as if this is goin' ter be difficult. We've got a dead man an' we know someone killed 'im, but there's jest nuthin' to suggest why or who. Did Gibbs have any relatives?'

'No, he was an orphan,' Peter answered.

'Married?' asked Mr. Budd hopefully.

Peter shook his head.

'No relatives, no wife, no nuthin'!' growled the superintendent disgustedly. 'Hm, come along; we'll get back ter Monk's Ferry an' see what that pub can rustle up in the way of a meal. I haven't had anythin' ter eat since me breakfast, an' I'm hungry.'

'So am I,' declared Sergeant Leek plaintively. 'Me stomach's stickin' to me backbone.'

Mr. Budd eyed his lean subordinate

disparagingly. 'Food's wasted on you,' he said. ''Owever much you ate, you'd always look like a streak of nuthin' with a lump o' gloom stuck on it.'

He took his leave of Superintendent Boyder, arranging to meet him on the following day and discuss the inquest, and started on the return journey to Monk's Ferry. As they left the outskirts of Barnford he turned to Peter, who was sitting beside him.

'Now,' he said, 'what about this precious information you was goin' ter give me? Let's have it.'

'All right.' Peter grinned. 'One of the things you want to know is what brought Lloyd Gibbs to Monk's Ferry, isn't it? Well, he came because of a woman!'

6

The Figure in the Moonlight

Eileen Shannon sat by the open window of her bedroom, staring out through the gathering dusk. There was a little vertical line between her level brows which had not been there on the previous day and which testified to the uneasiness of her thoughts. Since the moment when she had wakened with that horrible scream ringing in her ears, the peace and happiness of her life had been destroyed; for the big sleepy-eyed man who had come that afternoon had been right when he suggested that she had looked from her window in the night. She had looked, and in the clear moonlight had seen something that had swept away the foundations of her existence and left her a prey to nameless fears and terrors.

She had lied when the direct question had been put to her, and lied clumsily;

because if she had admitted looking out of the window, and declared she had seen nothing, the detective might have believed her. Now he very definitely did not believe her. He had made it quite obvious that he did not believe her. What would he do? She couldn't see that he could do very much. After all, there was no proof that she *had* looked out of that window — no proof that she had seen *anything*.

But now that he suspected that she had, wouldn't he try and find out what it was through some other source? By denying that she had done the obvious thing, she had as good as told him that she was concealing something. But her agitation and fear had numbed her brain and she had answered without thinking.

Perhaps after all it didn't matter very much. There had been nobody but herself to witness what she had seen, so how *could* he possibly find out? She tried to reassure herself that she had no cause for worry, but the effort was unsuccessful.

There came a tap on the door and she started violently, but it was only her mother who slipped into the room.

'How are you feeling now, dear? Is your head better?' inquired Mrs. Shannon solicitously. 'I don't think you ought to sit by that open window, do you? These nights get very chilly. I'm sure you'll catch a cold.'

'I'm quite warm, thank you, Mother.'

'I'm sure you'd be better in bed, dear,' persisted Mrs. Shannon, shaking her head. 'Will you let me send Bream up with something to eat? You've hardly eaten anything all day.'

'I don't want anything,' said Eileen wearily. All she wanted was to be left alone, but she couldn't very well say so.

'Just a glass of hot milk and a biscuit? You must eat something, dear, or you'll be really ill.'

'All right, Mother, I'll have some hot milk.' She was prepared to agree to anything if only her mother would stop fussing and go.

'We're all feeling the strain, I think,' said Mrs. Shannon. 'Your father's very touchy this evening, and Michael has scarcely said a word to anybody all day.'

'Where is he?'

'Curled up in a chair in the drawing-room reading a book. Your father has gone to his study to write letters. The whole house seems to have been upset by this dreadful thing, though none of us knew the man, so I can't think why it should.'

'It's because it happened so near,' said Eileen. She looked at the grey bulk of the ruined abbey that loomed indistinctly in the fading light. It had once been her favourite view. Now, she thought, she would never be able to look at it without horror and loathing.

'I never did like this house,' declared her mother surprisingly. 'I've always felt that there was something queer and unpleasant about it. Close to those horrible ruins, too. However much your father may ridicule the idea, I'm quite convinced that they *are* haunted, and I'm sure that they exercise an evil influence over the whole place.'

In spite of her trouble, Eileen smiled wanly. 'Nonsense, Mother. How could they — just a heap of old stones? And the house is a beautiful old place.'

'It may be very nice to look at,' said Mrs. Shannon doubtfully, 'but there's a nasty atmosphere about it. I'm sensitive to atmospheres.' This was an illusion she had fostered ever since a fortune-teller, who knew nothing about such things, had informed her that she was psychic. 'I'll go and order your hot milk, dear,' she said. 'Annie can bring it up, and if I were you I should go to bed and get some sleep. You look worn out.'

Eileen promised, and her mother kissed her good night and departed, to her relief. It was nearly dark now, and switching on the light she drew the curtains over the window. Perhaps if she could sleep she would feel better in the morning. She undressed and got into bed, trying to forget her uneasy thoughts in concentrating on a book.

Annie, the one maid whom the Shannons kept, and who, with the help of Bream and his wife and a daily woman from the village, did all the cleaning of the large house, brought her milk and a plate of biscuits. Eileen drank the hot milk gratefully, hoping that it might induce sleep; but, although her head ached with weariness, she had never felt more wakeful in her life.

She found herself reading the same page of her book over and over again without the least idea what it was about, and eventually put it down on the bedside table and lay staring at the ceiling, allowing the eager thoughts she had vainly attempted to keep at bay to come crowding back into her mind. Round and round they swung in endless circles, beginning where they left off, and ending where they began. The same thing over and over again.

She heard her mother come up the stairs, pass by her door, and go into her own bedroom. After a short interval she was followed by Michael. Her brother's footsteps hesitated as though he were going to stop at her door, but, after a moment, went on again and faded away as he mounted to the floor above. Presently — it was a long time after — she heard the study door open and close and her father's measured tread as he too went to his bedroom. The house was silent after that, and reaching out her arm Eileen switched out her bedside lamp and settled down to try and sleep.

The darkness soothed her burning eyes, but sleep seemed as far away as ever. She heard the muffled chime of the grandfather clock in the hall below strike midnight and then one o'clock. Somewhere in the trees round the house an owl hooted mournfully, and restlessly she turned over on her other side. Presently her thoughts began to fray into patches of blankness, and she was on the point of dropping asleep when she found herself suddenly wide awake again and listening. She wasn't quite sure what had wakened her, but something had.

The house was quite still. No sound of any sort reached her straining ears, and then she heard the clock chime two. Almost immediately afterward she heard another sound — the faint creaking of an opening door. In an instant she was sitting up in bed, her heart beating wildly.

The creaking sound came again. Somebody was up and moving about in the house below. It was the drawing-room door that creaked like that. Swiftly and silently she slid out of bed and pulled on a dressing-gown. Noiselessly she tiptoed over to the door and very quietly opened it.

The landing was in darkness. She listened, but she could hear nothing now. In her bare feet she moved towards the head of the stair, making no noise on the thick carpet, and leaned over the banister. The house below was in darkness, too, except for a brilliant shaft of moonlight that shone through a latticed window and patterned the polished parquet with lozenge-shaped lights. Almost breathlessly she stared down and listened. But there was no sound. And then she saw something move in the shadows — a blur of darkness that came into the patch of moonlight and took shape and substance.

She caught a glimpse of the long habit and the cowled head . . . Her scream shattered the silence of the house, like a stone crashing through a pane of glass, and then the darkness around her seemed to concentrate and clot in her brain and she slid to the floor . . .

7

The Burglary

Mr. Budd was usually a very early riser. When he was at home in his neat little villa in Streatham he invariably got up at six o'clock; and during the spring and summer months, when the exigencies of his profession allowed, he would spend two hours or so before breakfast pottering about his small garden among his beloved roses.

Although physically one of the laziest of men, he was mentally more alert than most, and his habitual lethargic exterior concealed one of the keenest brains in the C.I.D., as many had discovered to their cost. He held a theory that mental activity could only be brought to its highest degree if all bodily energy was conserved. In other words, the less you moved the more you could think — and as a direct result of this subjugation of all unnecessary muscular exercise, he had acquired his abnormal stoutness.

He awoke on the morning following his arrival at Monk's Ferry to find the sun streaming in through the latticed window of his bedroom and the hands of his watch pointing to three minutes to eight. Dismayed at the lateness of the hour, he sat up in bed, yawned, and rubbed his head vigorously. He had slept heavily and dreamlessly, and instead of feeling refreshed, he felt woolly and gummy-eyed. He put this down to the fact that he had slept too long, as he got ponderously out of bed and struggled into his dressing-gown. He had forgotten to ask them to call him and this was the result. He felt better when he had had a bath and shaved, and, dressing quickly, he went down to the coffee-room.

Peter Walton had reached the toast and marmalade stage of his breakfast when Mr. Budd joined him. 'Hello,' he greeted the superintendent cheerfully. 'You'll never be queen of the May if you keep these hours.'

Mr. Budd grunted. He was not feeling

in the mood for the reporter's facetiousness just then.

'I've got a lot o' serious work ter get through today,' he said irritably, 'so don't you start tryin' ter be funny, Walton.'

One of Mr. Jephcott's daughters — he had three and two sons — came to inquire if he was ready for breakfast and stopped the retort, concerning salts, which Peter was contemplating.

'I've been thinkin' over what you told me yesterday,' said Mr. Budd when the girl had gone, 'about Gibbs comin' here on account of some woman. If she was married or sump'n, it 'ud supply us with a motive.'

'I don't know whether she was married or single,' said Peter, shaking his head. 'I told you I don't know anything about her at all, except that Gibbs was crackers about her. He used to tell me quite a lot of things that he wouldn't have mentioned to anyone else, and this was one of 'em. But he never mentioned her name — only that she lived at Monk's Ferry.'

'Pity we haven't got her name,' murmured Mr. Budd musingly. 'You're sure he said she *lived* here an' not was *stayin'* here?'

'I think so,' answered Peter, 'but I wouldn't swear to it.'

'It makes a difference,' said the superintendent. 'If she was livin' here, we oughtn't have a lot of difficulty in findin' her. It's not a very big place.' He stopped and stared sleepily at the toast-rack.

'You're thinking it might be that woman at Abbotsway,' accused the reporter.

'Now what makes you think that?' inquired Mr. Budd innocently.

'Because it's obvious,' retorted the reporter impatiently. 'I had the same idea myself yesterday. She was keeping something back, and she was more agitated and nervous than she would have been if Gibbs had been a complete stranger.'

'I asked her if she knew 'im an' she said no,' broke in Mr. Budd gently.

'She said a lot of things that weren't true,' retorted Peter. 'You said that yourself. Why shouldn't she have been lying about Gibbs?'

'Maybe she was, an' then again, maybe

she wasn't. I don't like jumpin' ter conclusions. Sometimes yer find you've jumped inter somethin' that you can't get out of. There's no evidence at present to connect Miss Shannon with Gibbs.'

The arrival of Mr. Budd's breakfast interrupted the discussion for the moment. He eyed the laden dish of bacon and eggs with satisfaction. 'I will say one thin' fer these country pubs,' he murmured. 'They do feed you well.'

'Hm, you look as if you could do with some good solid food,' remarked Peter sarcastically. 'Reverting to the subject of this woman . . . '

But he was not destined to revert to it then, for the thin form of Sergeant Leek appeared at the door of the coffee-room, hovered uncertainly, caught sight of them, and shambled over to the table.

'Hello,' mumbled Mr. Budd, with his mouth full of bacon and egg. 'What do you want?'

'There's been a queer business up at that place Abbotsway durin' the night,' said the lugubrious Leek. 'I came ter tell yer. Fowler's up there now.'

'Queer business — what d'yer mean?'

'Somebody broke in an' scared the Shannon woman almost out of 'er wits. I don't know exac'ly what 'appened — only what Fowler told me, an' they didn't tell 'im much over the phone.'

'Nice, quiet, peaceful place this seems ter be,' remarked Mr. Budd. 'So somebody broke into Abbotsway an' frightened Miss Shannon, did they? Hm — interestin' an' peculiar. Did they steal anythin'?'

'I don't know. I tell yer, I dunno any o' the details.'

Mr. Budd attacked his breakfast, eating at a prodigious rate and speaking between mouthfuls. 'We'd better go up there an' find out,' he said. 'Sounds ter me as if this burglary might be important.'

'I don't see how it can have anything to do with Gibbs's murder,' interrupted Peter, frowning.

'You don't, eh?' grunted Mr. Budd. 'No more do I. But seein' that neither of us knows anythin' about the murder, except that there's a dead man at one end an' a killer at the other, it's impossible ter say, ain't it?' He gulped a cup of coffee noisily, wiped his lips on his napkin, and struggled to his feet, breathing heavily. 'We'll get along,' he said. 'There's no need fer you ter come, Walton.'

'Nothing short of battle, murder, and sudden death is going to keep me away,' declared Peter. 'Whither thou goest, I go! Lead on, Macduff!'

Mr. Budd went round to the garage, which had once been the stables, and got out his ancient car. Peter, with unpleasant memories of the previous drive to Abbotsway, elected to use his motorbike and travel in comparative comfort.

It was a lovely spring morning without a cloud in the sky, and the garden at Abbotsway was a concert hall filled with the joyous music of birds. Mr. Budd's noisy car shattered the melody like the intrusion of a machine-gun into a Haydn minuet as he drove it up the drive.

In the big house they found the large, and obviously perplexed, Constable Fowler laboriously taking notes in a black-covered book, with Bream and Colonel Shannon standing beside him. He welcomed their arrival with evident relief.

'I've got all the particulars 'ere, sir,' he said importantly, addressing Mr. Budd and tapping the notebook with his pencil, 'an' I've telephoned ter Barnford. The Sooper's on 'is way now. Entrance to the 'ouse was effected by the removal of a pane o' glass near the latch.'

'We'll go into all that presently,' broke in the superintendent. 'I'd like ter know first of all exac'ly what 'appened.'

'I can tell you that.' Colonel Shannon took a pace forward as he spoke. 'My daughter heard a noise in the night. Left her room and went to the head of the stairs to find out what it was. It seemed to have come from below. In the moonlight she saw somebody in the hall, screamed, and fainted.'

'Thank you, sir,' murmured Mr. Budd when the colonel stopped after this brief and rather staccato description of what had happened. 'Maybe your daughter could amplify that a little.'

'She can't see anybody,' declared the colonel, shaking his head. 'She's had a severe shock and is waiting for the doctor.'

'Hm.' Mr. Budd stroked his large nose gently. 'I'm sorry to hear that, sir. Well,' he added, shrugging his shoulders, 'maybe *you* can tell us a little more. F'rinstance, what was this noise that disturbed Miss Shannon?'

The colonel explained in his usual telegraphic style.

'I see.' The superintendent nodded slowly. 'An' this person she saw in the hall — was she able to give any description?'

'I've got it 'ere, sir,' Fowler, bursting with a desire to impart the information he had acquired, broke in eagerly. 'I've got it all 'ere.'

'Well, let's have it,' said Mr. Budd a little impatiently. 'Was it a man or a woman?'

There was a queer expression on the constable's face as he answered. 'You can't rightly tell, sir,' he said, 'not from the lady's description.'

'Pure imagination — that part of it,' interrupted the colonel shortly. 'Must have been. Or else some trick of the moonlight.'

'Whether it was imagination or a trick

o' the moonlight,' said Mr. Budd, quelling his exasperation with commendable fortitude, 'what was it she *said* she saw?'

'A monk, sir,' said Fowler.

Mr. Budd stared at him. 'D'you mean one o' these fellers from a monastery?'

'Yes, sir, accordin' to Miss Shannon's description. The person was dressed in a long robe with a cowl.'

'I'm convinced it was imagination,' said Colonel Shannon. 'All this nonsense they talk about . . . '

'What nonsense who talks about?' interrupted Mr. Budd quickly.

'A ridiculous legend of the neighbourhood,' snapped the colonel testily. 'A lot of rubbish about the ruins of the old abbey being haunted by the ghost of the abbot. Sheer stupidity!'

'There's a lot round 'ere what believes in it, sir,' put in Fowler stolidly. 'Though I'm not sayin' as 'ow I does meself,' he added hastily. There was no need for him to say so, thought Mr. Budd. His whole attitude more than suggested that he did.

'So there's a legend in the district about the ruins o' the abbey bein' haunted, is there?' murmured the super-intendent, frowning and fingering his chin. 'I should like to hear all about it.'

'I really can't see what it's got to do with this matter,' said Colonel Shannon irritably. 'But the story goes that when Henry's soldiers sacked Felsbank Abbey, they tortured and put to death the abbot. Since then his ghost is supposed to haunt the place. Absolute rubbish, of course!'

'Hm, I see,' said Mr. Budd slowly. 'Oh, well, if Miss Shannon saw somethin' that looked like this ghost, it's only natural that she'd be scared.'

'Imagination,' declared the colonel stubbornly.

'It wasn't all imagination,' said Mr. Budd, looking at him sleepily. 'She heard somethin' an' she saw somethin'. Maybe it wasn't a ghost, but it might o' been some-one who wanted people to think he was a ghost.' He yawned and turned to Fowler. 'Show me how this spook got in.'

The constable led the way into the drawing-room. A long, low casement window hung with chintz curtains and fitted with leaded panes of glass overlooked the garden. Near one of the old-fashioned iron catches a lozenge-shaped piece of glass had been neatly removed.

'The burglar's delight,' remarked Mr. Budd, peering at it. 'All you have ter do is push one o' these bits out, put in your hand an' pull the catch, an' you're in. It's as easy as havin' a key to the front door.'

He bent down and looked at the broad sill and the cushioned window-seat beneath it. There was a faint mark on the dark wood, and several indentations in the cushions. 'That's where he put his foot,' he murmured. 'An' there's a trace of mud on the floor.'

He pushed the window open wider, knelt on the seat, and leaned out. Immediately below was a narrow flower-bed, and in the loose earth the blurred marks of footprints.

'Well, that's how he came and that's how he went,' he muttered aloud to himself. 'The question is, what did he come for?'

'Anything of value that he could pick up,' said Colonel Shannon.

Mr. Budd pursed his lips and shook his

head doubtfully. 'I don't agree with you, sir. I don't think this feller who dressed himself up like a monk was just an ord'nary burglar. I think he came for some special object, an' I'd very much like ter know what it was.'

8

The Link

'Absolute nonsense, sir!' declared Colonel Shannon, making no effort to hide his annoyance. 'What possible object would there be?'

'I don't know,' Mr. Budd muttered, 'but I'm pretty sure there was somethin'. When you bought this house, did you buy all the contents as well?'

'Yes, with the exception of a few personal things belonging to the previous owner. But there's nothing here that anyone would want particularly. Your idea is absurd. This was just an ordinary burglar after whatever he could get.'

The superintendent sighed wearily. Colonel Shannon, having formed his opinion, was evidently determined that nothing was going to alter it. But Mr. Budd was convinced that he was right, and that the man of the night had been seeking something other than a few pieces of silver or such ordinary valuables as the house might offer.

The arrival of Superintendent Boyder put a temporary stop to all further discussion. He listened with interest to a description of what had happened, examined the meagre traces which the unknown had left behind him, frowned, and declared that he 'couldn't understand it'.

'It's easy enough to understand — up to a point,' growled Mr. Budd. 'Somebody dressed themselves up ter look like a monk an' broke in. The thing I want ter know is — what were they after, an' did they get it?'

'Is there anything missing, sir?' Boyder asked the colonel.

'Nothing,' Shannon answered. 'My daughter probably frightened the man before he could take anything.'

'That 'ud appear to be the size of it, sir,' agreed the local man. 'Well, there doesn't seem to have been much harm done — except the shock to your daughter, sir. I expect it was just some tramp who thought he might pick up somethin' of value.'

'Do tramps usually wander about this part of the country dressed as monks?' demanded Mr. Budd sarcastically.

'The lady could have been mistaken about that,' said Boyder. 'I understand the hall was in darkness except for a bit of moonlight, an' if this feller had been wearin' a coat that was too big for him . . . Well, a little bit of imagination 'ud do the rest, wouldn't it?'

'Quite right,' interposed Colonel Shannon. 'Exactly what I said myself.'

Mr. Budd refrained from further argument. He had his own ideas on the subject, and possibly time would prove who was right. He would have liked to have had a word with Eileen Shannon, but there seemed no likelihood of it at the moment. No doubt an interview could be arranged with her later. In the meanwhile, he had plenty to occupy his mind.

They took their departure soon after, Boyder going back to Barnford, and Mr. Budd, Leek, and Peter Walton returning to The Monk's Head.

'They might just as well have let you eat your breakfast in peace,' remarked the reporter when they reached the inn. 'That little effort was a sheer waste of time.'

'I don't think it was,' grunted Mr. Budd.

Peter looked at him curiously. 'Why? Surely you don't think it can have any connection with Gibbs's murder . . . ?'

'That's the second time you've said the same thin',' snapped Mr. Budd irritably, 'an' I'm goin' ter tell you somethin'. I think this business at Abbotsway has got a lot ter do with Gibbs's murder, but don't go askin' me why. It's just a hunch o' mine.'

He lumbered heavily away. Peter watched him until he disappeared inside the inn and then turned to Leek. 'What's he getting at?' he said thoughtfully.

'Don't ask me,' Leek remarked gloomily. 'I never know what 'e's gettin' at.' He blinked wearily. 'I might as well go back ter the cottage an' 'ave a bit of rest. 'E don't seem ter want me fer anythin', an' I didn't sleep none too well last night.'

He shuffled mournfully away, and Peter

went in search of a telephone to dictate to an eager and impatient, and ultimately disappointed, news editor the meagre results of his inquiry into the death of Lloyd Gibbs.

Mr. Budd, yawning and looking completely bored, sought out the genial Mr. Jephcott. He found that worthy man taking his ease in a deck-chair in the garden; and having lighted one of his thin black cigars, proceeded to extract in his own slow, roundabout fashion certain information which he concluded the landlord possessed. He began by discussing the garden, then led the conversation carefully and skilfully to the age of the inn, and from thence to the past history of Monk's Ferry. 'There's some sort of legend attached to the ruins o' the old abbey, they tell me,' he murmured, puffing out a cloud of acrid smoke. 'Somethin' about a ghost, ain't it?'

Mr. Jephcott nodded his shining head. 'You mean the Felsbank Abbot,' he said. 'That story's been going around for a good many 'undred years now, an' there's still a lot of people in these parts who believe in it. I've never come across anyone who's ever actually seen anything, but my great-grandfather's s'posed to have known a man what did — an' died from a stroke afterwards.'

'Is this spook s'posed ter be so terrifyin'?' Mr. Budd inquired.

The landlord smiled. 'According to all accounts he *is* pretty fearsome. The story goes that after King Henry's men had put him to torture because he refused to reveal where he had hidden the wealth of the abbey, he was so dreadful to look upon that no mortal eye could bear the sight. He was a game old chap, though, because he died from his injuries without telling 'em what they wanted to know.' He stopped and regarded Mr. Budd with a slight twinkle in his eyes. 'You wouldn't be thinkin' that the ghost of the old abbot 'ad anything to do with this murder, would you?'

'No, I wouldn't be thinkin' that,' Mr. Budd said slowly. 'But I've known ghosts ter be very useful at times. People don't inquire too closely into somethin' they think might be a ghost.'

Mr. Jephcott's shrewd eyes expressed his complete understanding. 'I see what you mean. Perhaps Mr. Gibbs wasn't superstitious and inquired *too* closely. I've wondered quite a lot what it was that took 'im to those ruins in the middle of the night. Maybe he was looking for the Twelve Apostles . . . '

The cigar fell from Mr. Budd's mouth and hit the ground with a little shower of sparks. 'What did you say?' he demanded sharply.

'The Twelve Apostles,' repeated Mr. Jephcott in a tone of surprise. 'Felsbank Abbey was noted for them. They were life-size statues of the twelve apostles in solid silver, and they used to occupy niches in the Great Hall. It was because the abbot wouldn't say where he had hidden them that Henry's soldiers tortured him. They couldn't find 'em and they never have been found.'

Mr. Budd listened, and as he listened the sun-filled garden of The Monk's Head faded and was replaced by the picture of a wet and dreary November night. He was standing beside a narrow bed, and in his imagination could hear the laboured breathing of a dying man and the disjointed words he uttered as his life ebbed swiftly away.

'   . . . a million quid . . . the Twelve Apostles . . . '

'Worth over a million pounds, they're s'posed to be.' The voice of Mr. Jephcott drowned the phantom whisper of that other voice. 'Though where they was hid nobody knows. Quite a lot of these archaeologist chaps 'ave had a shot at tryin' to find 'em at various times, but none of 'em 'as been lucky.'

The superintendent had recovered from his surprise. 'That's very interestin' — very interestin' indeed. Twelve solid silver statues of the apostles hidden somewhere in the district an' nobody knows where. Hm, this abbot feller must've been pretty clever.'

'They were cunning old chaps, the monks,' said Mr. Jephcott with a wink. 'Well, I must go and tap a fresh barrel, sir.' He got up, stretched himself, and went into the inn. Mr. Budd walked slowly and ponderously in the wake of the landlord and made his way upstairs to his room. He wanted to be alone and think.

Locking the door he took off his jacket, hung it carefully over the back of a chair, and lay down on the bed. This was his invariable custom when he wanted to sort his ideas, and he had found that many a stiff problem yielded to this system of complete bodily comfort and induced mental concentration. Shifting the pillows to a comfortable support for his head, he lighted another cigar and, letting his muscles relax, closed his eyes and began a careful review of the situation.

The death of little Lew Cator, which had not been an accident, was very definitely connected with Monk's Ferry. The cryptic words he had uttered before he died, and which had puzzled the superintendent, could only refer to the silver statues of the twelve apostles which the monks had hidden to prevent them falling into the hands of Henry's men, and which, according to Mr. Jephcott, had never been found. It was ridiculous to suppose that such a thing could only be a coincidence. There had been something else the little crook had said — something about an Abbot's Key, which tended still further to make all thoughts of a coincidence ridiculous. No, there was, without any doubt at all, a link between the death of Lew and this hidden treasure of Felsbank Abbey. The question was, was there also a link with the murder of Lloyd Gibbs? Was the man who had run down Lew Cator in his car on that wet November night also responsible for the killing of Gibbs? If so, why had he killed the reporter? Lew Cator, judging from what he had managed to say, had been killed because he refused to get or steal a key — the Abbot's Key. But what was the motive for the murder of Gibbs? Had he been killed because he had discovered something that was dangerous to this unknown man's safety? If there was any connection between his death and Lew Cator and the Twelve Apostles, this seemed a plausible theory.

The ash from Mr. Budd's cigar fell on the capacious bulge of his waistcoat as he raised a hand and removed it from his lips. That was the crux of the whole thing:

what was there to discover? The murderer of Lew Cator had obviously found a clue to the whereabouts of the twelve silver saints so long hidden in the vicinity of Monk's Ferry — a clue that presumably had something to do with the acquiring of the Abbot's Key. Lew had refused to get this and had been killed as a consequence; therefore it was natural to suppose that the unknown had been forced to adopt other methods, and the reason behind them had come to the knowledge of Lloyd Gibbs. The reporter had had many contacts among what was loosely described as the underworld, and it was not difficult to imagine that a stray word spoken in an obscure club might have aroused his natural curiosity and put him on the track.

This, of course, was all conjecture, and there were a lot of loose ends floating about, such as the reason for Eileen Shannon's queer behaviour, but it was at least something to build on. Mr. Budd realized that he would have to amend and revise his ideas several times before he really got at the truth. It had been something of a shock to find that the starting-point in this case was little Lew Cator, whose death and unintelligible words he had almost forgotten, although experience should have taught him that such things were by no means uncommon. It had happened to him over and over again — an incident, a vague remark — not understood at all until sometime later, and then recalled and dropped neatly into place to complete a pattern.

Not that this completed any pattern; it only began one. But some kind of nebulous shape was there — ghostly and indistinct, like the gradual uncovering of a palimpsest, but definitely there. Lew had been an expert burglar, and his murderer had wanted him to get the Abbot's Key. There had been a burglary at Abbotsway. Was it jumping to conclusions too much to suppose that the unknown man who had broken in had been seeking the Abbot's Key? And if so, what *was* the Abbot's Key? Perhaps Colonel Shannon could supply the answer to that, if he were asked. And the superintendent decided that he *would* be asked at the first available opportunity.

9

Introducing 'Spooky' Withers

There were more people in the bar than there had been on the previous day. The three men who looked like farmers were back again drinking pints of beer and talking in low tones. The man with a newspaper was there, too, sitting at the same table; and there were several men grouped together with whom Mr. Jephcott was carrying on an animated conversation, probably local tradesmen.

Of the woman who had awakened that elusive memory in Mr. Budd's mind there was no sign, but in her place was a stout red-faced man in ginger-coloured plus-fours with very smoothly brushed hair almost the same colour as his suit, but flecked with grey. He had a tiny smear of moustache, and eyes of a pale blue which bulged, and taken in conjunction with rather high brows, gave him a permanent expression of surprise.

Lying on the floor beside him and surveying the entire assembly with contemptuous boredom was a large bull terrier. Mr. Budd had expected to find Peter Walton, but the reporter was either refreshing himself elsewhere or had taken himself off on some expedition of his own.

Mr. Jephcott detached himself from his cronies long enough to draw the superintendent a tankard of beer, and then went back to his discussion. Mr. Budd drank his beer in thoughtful solitude. He had decided not to say anything to Peter, as yet anyway, about the result of his morning's cogitation. There would be time enough for that when he had collected more facts. In the meanwhile, the fewer people who knew about Lew Cator and his connection with the affair, the better, for a chance word might reach the ears of the prime mover in the matter and put him on his guard.

He was lazily contemplating his second pint and deciding that the beer at The Monk's Head was very good indeed, when a man came into the bar, strode up to the counter and rapped with the edge of a coin to attract Mr. Jephcott's attention. The sound, if it had no immediate effect on Mr. Jephcott, caused Mr. Budd to look up and eye the newcomer with a certain amount of astonishment. He was very tall and very lean, with a mass of iron-grey hair that was swept back from his forehead and fell untidily over the back of his collar. His face was long and thin, shaped rather like a calabash pear, and his tight-lipped mouth drooped at the corners with deeply engraved lines that ran up to meet his large, high-bridged nose, on which was set a pair of gold-rimmed pince-nez. He was dressed in a very baggy and shapeless suit of clerical grey flannel, and wore a high black stock. His whole appearance suggested a rather seedy actor of the old school.

'A double Haig, if you please,' he said in a precise tenor when he had at last succeeded in attracting the landlord's attention, 'and a baby Polly, if you have one.'

Mr. Jephcott supplied his needs without haste, took the coins he tendered, gave him his change, and returned to his friends.

The interested Mr. Budd moved along the bar until he reached the newcomer's side. 'Well, well,' he murmured softly. 'If it isn't 'Spooky' Withers. I thought you was still 'inside', Spooky?'

The lean man started and almost spilled the soda-water he was pouring into his whisky. Setting the little bottle down, he peered at Mr. Budd over the top of his glass. 'Oh, it's you,' he grunted ungraciously. 'What are you doing here?'

'Drinkin' beer,' replied the superintendent truthfully. 'What brings you to Monk's Ferry?'

Mr. Withers took a large sip of whisky and soda and swallowed it noisily. 'Why shouldn't I come here if I want to?' he demanded. 'It's a free country, isn't it?'

'It is,' agreed Mr. Budd heartily. 'Though your freedom has been a bit spasmodic, Spooky. When did they let you out?'

'If,' the lean man said with great

dignity, 'you are referring to the gross miscarriage of justice that resulted in my incarceration in Wormwood Scrubbs, last week.'

'You do it beautifully,' remarked Mr. Budd admiringly, and gulped his beer. 'I s'pose the time before was a gross miscarriage of justice, too, eh?'

'It most certainly was. I have suffered a great deal from police persecution.' He finished his whisky and called for another.

'Goin' in fer expensive drinks, too,' murmured the detective. 'So you're in the money, Spooky. Whose money are you in this time?'

'You mind your own business,' the other snapped angrily.

'It'll be my business sooner or later,' said Mr. Budd gently. 'Well, well. It's interestin' an' peculiar meetin' you here. Did you know Lloyd Gibbs?' He shot the question suddenly, watching to see the effect it had. A wary look came into Mr. Withers's eyes — a cautious expression that seemed to say, *This is where I must tread very carefully.*

'Lloyd Gibbs? Who's he?'

You know very well who Lloyd Gibbs was, thought Mr. Budd, and said, 'He isn't anybody. He's dead. He was murdered.'

'Why should I know anything about him?' Mr. Withers demanded suspiciously. 'Are you suggesting — '

'I'm not suggestin' anythin',' broke in the superintendent. 'I just asked you a simple question, that's all.'

'I don't like your damned questions,' grunted Mr. Withers, pouring the remainder of his soda-water into the fresh double Haig which the landlord had brought. 'You've got nothing on me, Budd, and don't you try and fix anything. I'm at liberty to go where I like without asking permission of any flat-footed, thick-skulled policeman.'

'Of course you are,' murmured Mr. Budd mildly. 'An' nobody's tryin' to stop you — not yet.'

Mr. Withers muttered something that was probably extremely uncomplimentary below his breath.

Mr. Budd drank the remainder of his beer and set the empty tankard down on the counter. 'Well, I'll be gettin' along, Spooky,' he said. 'I've no doubt we'll be seein' each other again pretty soon. Don't go gettin' into trouble.'

The superintendent left the bar and made his way to the coffee-room for lunch. While he ate the meal, he pondered over this latest development. What had brought Spooky Withers to Monk's Ferry? His arrival in that ancient village was surely no coincidence. Spooky's appearance was part of the unknown scheme of things, but what part? Mr. Budd did not imagine that he had personally participated in the murder of Lloyd Gibbs, but he probably knew who was responsible, and the reason why the reporter had been killed.

Spooky Withers was rather out of the ordinary run of crooks. He had started life as a schoolmaster, and had drifted onto the stage. After a precarious existence touring the country playing small parts, he had suddenly blossomed forth as a spiritualist, and this was the beginning of his downfall. Whether he had any genuine aptitude as a medium was a moot point, but his activities in this direction served as a very excellent cloak for a profitable form of blackmail, and he was making a very lucrative living when the police stepped in and put a temporary stop to his spiritual researches.

When he came out after serving the fairly stiff sentence which a sceptical judge had passed on him, he returned to the fray neither chastened nor abashed. In six months he was standing again in the dock listening to certain biographical details expounded by an unimaginative prosecuting counsel that left him under no misapprehension regarding his character. This time the judge sent him down for three years, a sentence which he had served in Wormwood Scrubbs, and from which he could only, even allowing for the usual remission for good conduct, have just been released.

And now here he was in Monk's Ferry, looking anything but prosperous, but apparently in possession of a certain amount of money, and no doubt for the purpose of acquiring more as speedily as possible. Had he heard of the hidden treasure of Felsbank Abbey and was hoping to cash in on it? Mr. Budd concluded, from what he knew of Spooky Withers, that it was unlikely. The treasure, if indeed its existence was factual and not merely legendary, would take a certain amount of time to find and turn into cash. Withers would be after something that was quicker and more certain. His speciality had always been blackmail, and it was Mr. Budd's experience that crooks rarely changed their methods. It was a great deal more likely that he was out to cash in on something he knew concerning the person or persons responsible for the killing of Gibbs.

If in some queer way he had discovered the identity of the murderer of the reporter and little Lew Cator, he was in possession of knowledge that was definitely of considerable cash value. And if he knew this, he was also of considerable value to the police. All things considered, Mr. Budd had decided by the time he had finished his meal that Spooky Withers was deserving of a great deal of attention.

Peter Walton had not put in an

appearance by the time he left the coffee-room, which rather surprised him, but he concluded that the reporter was out on some investigation of his own which he would probably hear all about when they eventually met. In the meanwhile he decided to satisfy his curiosity regarding the Abbot's Key and made his way to the garage for his car.

On the way he passed through the bar, which was by now almost empty. Only Mr. Jephcott and two of the men who looked like local tradesmen remained. The big man wondered where Spooky Withers had gone and rather regretted that he had not kept an eye on him. However, he would be pretty easy to find if he was wanted, and he had a hunch that wherever he had gone it was not far away.

It was a lovely afternoon, and with one of his thin black cigars stuck between his teeth and an excellent lunch inside his capacious stomach, Mr. Budd enjoyed the drive to Abbotsway. Colonel Shannon was sitting in the garden reading when the superintendent arrived, and made no secret of his dislike at having his peace so rudely disturbed.

He frowned at Mr. Budd's question and shook his head. 'Abbot's Key?' he repeated. 'Don't know what the devil you're talking about. Never heard of it.'

He repeated his assertion in spite of all the detective's persistence, and eventually got so red in the face that Mr. Budd gave it up and tactfully withdrew. He left with the impression that the colonel had spoken the truth.

Mr. Budd drove slowly back, not a little disappointed with the result of his visit. He had expected to find a key at Abbotsway, and Colonel Shannon's failure to substantiate that expectation necessitated the rearranging of his ideas, for without a key — known as the Abbot's Key — his theory regarding the motive for the previous night's burglary fell to the ground. He wondered whether he was allowing his imagination to run away with him.

And yet the silver Twelve Apostles were no figments of his imagination. They existed, or had existed, and their existence had been known to Lew Cator

— and not only their existence but their value. And the Abbot's Key was in some way definitely connected with them. Lew had been asked to get it and had refused, and because of his refusal he had been run down and injured so badly that he had died.

There *must* be an Abbot's Key. Perhaps his mistake had been in supposing it to be at Abbotsway. Or was it there, unknown to Colonel Shannon and his family, but known to the man who had come in the night?

Weary and a little irritable, Mr. Budd swung the car out of a side lane and almost knocked down three people and a dog who were walking slowly along the main road. They scattered quickly as he drove past, and the dog barked angrily. The little group comprised Spooky Withers, the red-faced man in ginger-coloured plus-fours, and the woman whose face had stirred that illusive memory in Mr. Budd's mind on the previous day. All three of them together, and obviously well known to each other. Here was something fresh to chew on.

Spooky Withers had come to Monk's Ferry to meet these two. Yet the red-faced man had given him no sign of recognition in the bar at The Monk's Head. Who was that man, and who was the woman? And where had the superintendent seen her before?

He drove on mechanically, his mind trying vainly to pin down that stray memory and supply it with a background. And suddenly, just as The Monk's Head came in sight, there rose before his eyes the picture of a crowded court and of a man in the dock . . .

That's where he had seen her. At the trial of Everitt Marie four years ago.

10

Mr. Budd is Puzzled

The inquest into the death of Lloyd Gibbs took place at Barnford on the following morning and was neither interesting nor protracted. Peter Walton supplied evidence of identification, Doctor Lidstone gave his opinion concerning the cause of death — of which nobody ever had any possible doubt, and then Superintendent Boyder asked for and was granted a fortnight's adjournment. The little courtroom in which the proceedings took place was crowded, and every London newspaper was represented. But, although Mr. Budd searched, there was no sign of Spooky Withers, the red-faced man, or the mysterious woman.

A question to Mr. Jephcott had supplied the name of the red-faced man. He was a Major Snodland and lived at a small cottage in Monk's Ferry called

Abbot's Rest — it was queer, thought Mr. Budd, how nearly everything in the district was either an Abbot or a Monk's something — and had lived there for nearly two years. The landlord volunteered the information that he was not very popular in the neighbourhood, but gave no particular reason for this. It was generally believed that he had a private income and was quite well off, and this belief was based on the fact that he spent most of his time playing golf and walking aimlessly about the countryside with his dog, who rejoiced in the unusual name of Bisto. Mr. Jephcott, now well into his stride, had added a further item with great relish — to wit, that the attractive lady who had been in the bar when Mr. Budd had arrived, and whom he had asked about, was staying with Major Snodland. The major had told Mrs. Blimber, who 'did' for him, and who had apparently told the entire inhabitants of Monk's Ferry that the lady was his sister — a Mrs. Rita Claydon. But Mrs. Blimber and all the inhabitants of Monk's Ferry seemed to have considerable doubts about the truth of this, and to be properly shocked in consequence, since Major Snodland was a bachelor, and before the advent of his guest had lived entirely alone. Mrs. Blimber had further confided to all the inhabitants of Monk's Ferry that she thought it 'corrupting to the morals', though whose morals were likely to be corrupted, unless they were the dog Bisto's, Mr. Budd was unable to see.

But he had added to his stock of information, though the addition did not get him very far. The actual status of Mrs. Claydon in Major Snodland's household did not interest him at all, though he was inclined to agree with the suspicions of Mrs. Blimber and all the inhabitants of Monk's Ferry on the subject. What did interest him tremendously was his accidental discovery that both she and the florid-faced Snodland were friendly with Spooky Withers. It seemed to him that these three were engaged in some project together that was very closely connected with the murder of Lloyd Gibbs, though exactly what that project was he was unable to conjecture. That it had something to do with the Twelve Apostles appeared to be almost certain, but what?

Not in his wildest imaginings did he come within measurable distance of even the fringe of the true reason for Spooky Withers's presence in Monk's Ferry, and his association with the attractive Mrs. Claydon and the tenant of Abbot's Rest. Had he done so, he could have prevented quite a lot of trouble for a number of people, and most certainly saved the life of one who died trying to satisfy a very understandable curiosity.

Mr. Budd came back from Barnford in company with Sergeant Leek, for Peter Walton had elected to stay behind and drink with the other reporters from Fleet Street. The superintendent had been invited to join their gathering — an invitation which he tactfully declined, guessing that it was prompted by a desire to apply a little gentle prodding for information, and being determined that he was not going to be prodded. It was all too hazy and theoretical to discuss with anyone at present — with the possible exception of Leek, and Mr. Budd had long since ceased to regard the gloomy sergeant as being anyone. His personality was so completely negative that Mr. Budd could set forth the salient points of a case, and his deductions therefrom, without fear of argument, and found on occasions that this was a great help in clarifying his ideas. Talking to Leek served to frame his train of thought, although once or twice his not very intelligent comments had supplied a new angle.

This morning, however, as they bumped and jolted along the road from Barnford to Monk's Ferry, the superintendent was in no mood to discuss the case with even his misanthropic subordinate. His mind was too chaotic. The few pieces of the puzzle which he possessed refused to join together into anything like a coherent pattern.

His remembrance of where he had seen Mrs. Claydon before had started a fresh hare which he found very difficult to catch. Had she been in the court out of sheer idle curiosity, or had she been there because she took a personal interest in Everitt Marie? Finding her at Monk's

111

Ferry seemed to suggest that she had known Marie. It was at Abottsway that Marie had been arrested. This opened up a basis for new speculation. Marie had been the owner of Abbotsway before Colonel Shannon; therefore it was not an impossible supposition that the whole train of events had started with him. Mr. Budd decided that he would like to know more about Everitt Marie, his activities and background. Perhaps here was to be found the clue that would make everything clear.

'Do you remember anything about the Marie case?' he asked Sergeant Leek. 'Everitt Marie, the financier.'

'Marie,' muttered Leek, knitting his brows without the faintest idea of ever having heard of Marie before in his life. 'Now let me see . . . '

'If you don't know anythin' about him, why don't you say so,' snapped Mr. Budd irritably. 'It's no good makin' faces.'

The unfortunate Leek was forced to admit that he could not recall anything about Everitt Marie. ''As 'e got anythin' ter do with this business?' he inquired.

'If he hadn't, should I be askin' about him. Use your common sense.'

The sergeant, who had been desperately endeavouring to do so, and always found it a very difficult operation, sighed and looked even more melancholy than usual. 'I always seem ter say the wrong thing,' he remarked in an injured tone.

Mr. Budd grunted. 'You can't help it, I s'pose. Anyway, this feller Marie was a big financier. He controlled several companies an' was worth thousands an' thousands o' pounds, only he wasn't satisfied an' wanted more. He did a bit o' fiddlin' with some shares, an' there was a bust-up an' he was arrested an' sentenced to four years' penal servitude an' died in prison a few months back.'

'Oh, 'e's dead, is 'e,' said Leek when Mr. Budd paused for breath. 'Well if he's dead, I don't see 'ow 'e could be mixed up with this job.'

'You couldn't see a thousand candle-power floodlight stuck on the end o' your nose,' growled Mr. Budd disparagingly. 'Don't you know what Shakespeare says about 'the evil of men livin' after 'em'?'

He always attributed his quotations to Shakespeare, and ninety-nine times out of a hundred he was right.

'Is 'e mixed up in it, too?' asked the sergeant.

'Shakespeare's dead!' snarled Mr. Budd.

'Well then 'ow can 'e — ' began the bewildered sergeant.

'Shakespeare was a feller who wrote plays,' broke in his exasperated superior, 'years an' years ago. Don't you know anythin'? What did they teach you at school . . . ?' He broke off, slammed on the brakes, and brought the ancient car to such a sudden and unexpected stop that the unfortunate Leek was nearly projected headfirst through the windscreen. Not unreasonably annoyed, he had opened his mouth to protest against this behaviour on the part of his superior when he saw the cause. Coming along the road towards them was a woman, and he recognized Eileen Shannon. She had apparently been down to the village on a shopping expedition, for she carried a basket laden with parcels. As she drew nearer, he saw that she was looking pale and wan; and when she saw whom the car contained, a startled look came into her eyes and she almost stopped.

'I want a word with this woman,' said Mr. Budd under his breath. 'You stay where you are.'

Leek nodded ruefully and rubbed his forehead, which had come in violent contact with the glass screen. The superintendent opened the door and got out. As Eileen approached, he went to meet her.

'Good mornin', miss,' he greeted pleasantly. 'I hope you've quite recovered from that shock you 'ad?'

'Yes, thank you,' she said, though her looks belied her.

'Nasty experience,' murmured Mr. Budd sympathetically, 'comin' on the top o' the other, too.'

She dropped her eyes. 'What — what other?' she asked.

'Why, on the night of the murder, miss,' said Mr. Budd. 'When you heard the scream.'

'Oh, yes, that.' He could have sworn there was relief in her voice. 'It was dreadful . . . '

She was nervous and ill at ease, anxious to terminate the interview and be on her way. But Mr. Budd had other ideas and planted his huge bulk in her path, so that without being deliberately rude she could not pass. 'It must have been very unpleasant, miss,' he said, shaking his head. 'Enough to scare anyone. Murder's a nasty business at any time, but when it happens outside your window, so to speak — well . . . ' After a pause, he went on thoughtfully: 'There was somebody in your garden that night. If we can find out who it was, I think we'll have got the murderer.'

Her face went white and the startled fear in her eyes deepened. 'There wasn't . . . ' she began quickly, and hastily corrected herself. 'How do you know?'

Mr. Budd did not know. His assertion had been a shot in the dark fired with the express purpose of seeing what reaction his statement would produce, and he was quite satisfied with the result.

'We have ways an' means of findin' out these things, miss,' he answered a little vaguely. 'Pity you didn't look out o' the window after you heard the scream. You'd have seen this feller, an' you could 'ave given us some idea what he looked like.'

'I don't see how you can be sure there was anybody,' she answered. 'Did anyone see him?'

'I'm afraid I can't answer that, miss,' muttered the superintendent. 'But you can take it from me there was someone. *And you know very well there was*, he thought as he watched her, *because I'll bet you were lookin' out o' that window*.

'Why should anyone want to come into our garden?' she asked unexpectedly. 'The ruins are on the other side of the old riverbed. I can't see any reason why anyone should come into our garden at all.'

'That rather puzzled me, miss,' said Mr. Budd, unable to think of any other answer to this question. 'Unless this feller was the same one who broke in the other night. I've been wantin' to ask you if you can give any sort of a description of the man you saw in the hall. Was he short, tall? Anythin' about 'im that'd help us to identify him?'

'No; I only caught a second's glimpse of him as he came into the moonlight. He was wearing the robe and cowl of a monk. I can't tell you what he was like or anything about him except that.'

There was a difference in her manner which he noticed at once. It was more decisive, and the hesitancy in her speech that had almost amounted to a stammer was gone. Regarding the man she had seen in the night, she was telling the truth. It was only about that other night — the night of Lloyd Gibbs's murder — that she was lying, and lying so clumsily that it was obvious.

'You haven't heard any mention of somethin' called the Abbot's Key, have you, miss?' he asked.

She shook her head. 'No. Why? What is it?'

'I don't know exactly what it is,' said Mr. Budd truthfully. 'I s'pose it's some sort of a key, though I can't be certain of that. I just wondered if you'd ever heard of it.'

'Nearly everything is called the Abbot's something or other round here,' she said with a ghost of a smile, 'but I've never heard of the Abbot's Key. There's a big square rock in our garden called Abbot's Stone, and there's a gate in the wall which is known as the Abbot's Gate . . . '

'Has that got a key to it?' asked the detective quickly.

'Not now. It may have had at one time — there's a huge old-fashioned lock, but it doesn't work. We use the bolts.' She glanced at the watch on her wrist. 'I really must go. Some of the things I have in this basket are wanted for lunch. Goodbye.'

Mr. Budd stepped aside and watched her as she hurried up the road. What did she know that she was trying so badly to conceal, and why should she conceal anything? There was only one answer to that. She, too, was mixed up in this queer business which involved the death of Lew Cator, the murder of Lloyd Gibbs, and twelve solid silver statues of the apostles worth a million pounds.

11

Concerning the Late Mr. Marie

What Mr. Budd afterwards referred to as the second phase of the Monk's Ferry Mystery did not begin until three days after the inquest, and during the intervening period very little happened at all, although the superintendent himself was by no means idle.

Sergeant Leek, to his undisguised chagrin, was given the job of watching Abbot's Rest and its three inhabitants — for Spooky Withers had taken up his abode in the Snodland household — and found this occupation both boring and unprofitable. All three conducted themselves with exemplary rectitude; their lives, so far as the weary Leek could testify, being as blameless and unblemished as an archbishop's. They went for walks, they played golf, and they retired early. There was nothing which by the very greatest stretch of the imagination could have been regarded as suspicious.

'I'm just wastin' me time,' complained the gloomy sergeant during one of his completely negative reports to Mr. Budd. 'They go on like a bloomin' Sunday school treat.'

'Just go on wastin' yer time,' said his superior. 'Withers isn't stayin' here for his health. There's somethin' brewin', an' sooner or later it'll start boilin' over.'

'The whole business looks like petering out,' said Peter Walton disgustedly, after he had discussed the case with the superintendent. 'I can't discover anything.'

Mr. Budd only grunted. He had no intention of saying anything about his own ideas on the subject, although his reticence made the reporter suspicious.

'I believe you've got something at the back of your mind,' he accused.

'Maybe I have an' maybe I haven't,' the superintendent said noncommittally, and left it at that.

On the second day he went to London, leaving Monk's Ferry after an early breakfast, and he did not return until the following afternoon. He occupied part of his time at Scotland Yard, going carefully through the file containing the records of the Everitt Marie case, but he found very little indeed to reward him for his labours.

Marie's career had been spectacular and meteoric. From comparative obscurity — very little seemed to be known about his origins — he had suddenly blazed across the financial firmaments, scattering a golden trail in his wake. Everything he touched had been successful. He had become a leading power in the world, and every big financial project had Marie somewhere connected with it.

He had amassed a colossal fortune, and two years before his arrest could have retired with almost fabulous riches. And then things had gone wrong. His gigantic speculations had tottered, and in a desperate attempt to save the whole elaborate structure from falling he had used not only all his own money, but had forged and converted share certificates that were not his. If he could have avoided discovery for another six months, he might have been able to save everything by this dubious financial juggling, but a man whom he trusted had got scared, lost his nerve, and blown the gaff.

Almost before Marie had time to turn round, the crash came, and he found himself arrested for fraud. Nothing could save him after that, for an investigation into his affairs, and the affairs of the numerous companies he controlled, brought to light evidence of his guilt that was indisputable. A broken man without one penny of his enormous fortune left, he went to Wormwood Scrubbs to serve a sentence of four years; and two months before he was due to be released, contracted pneumonia and died in the prison infirmary.

Mr. Budd interviewed the lawyers who had acted for Marie, but they could add very little to what he already knew. Abbotsway had been sold with its contents to Colonel Shannon, and the money had gone to help defray the huge legal costs of the trial. Marie's family had consisted only of his wife and one daughter. The former had died a year after his arrest, and the latter, who had married before her father's disgrace, had gone to live with her husband in New York, and so far as was known was still living there. The lawyers could give no information about Mrs. Claydon. They knew nothing about her at all, and had apparently never even heard of her.

Disgruntled and irritated at his complete inability to find anything to link the Marie case with the murder of Lloyd Gibbs, Mr. Budd wearily tried Wormwood Scrubbs. The governor, a patient man and most anxious to help, supplied one small item of information which Mr. Budd filed away in the recesses of his mind as of possible future value. Marie, on the day before he died, had requested to see somebody by the name of Jackson. His request, since it was obvious that he was dying, was granted, and the man had been sent for. He came, and was with Marie for only a few minutes. He could have remained longer, but Marie, who was very ill by then, had lapsed into a coma from which he never recovered, and the doctor, who was hastily summoned, thought it inadvisable that the visitor should stay. The governor could give only the vaguest description of this man Jackson, and was unable to remember the address which Marie had given. It was somewhere in Brixton, but that was all he could recollect.

Mr. Budd returned to Monk's Ferry little wiser than when he had left. He arrived in the late afternoon, hot, weary, dusty, and aching after his long journey in the bone-shaking rattletrap which he dignified by the name of car.

He was washing in his room at The Monk's Head when there was a tap on the door, and Sergeant Leek intruded his long lean form. 'Oh, you've got back, 'ave yer?' he said unnecessarily.

Mr. Budd raised a red and dripping face from the wash-basin and groped blindly for a towel. 'No,' he spluttered dispiritedly as he rubbed himself dry, 'I 'aven't got back. This isn't me . . . What d'you want?'

Leek stumbled further into the room, closed the door, and leaned against the frame. 'Thought I'd just come an' tell you that nothin's 'appened while you've been away,' he said mournfully. 'I arranged with a feller from Barnford to relieve me, an' we've kept them people under a close watch between us, but nothin's 'appened.'

'That's very interestin',' Mr. Budd said crossly, 'very helpful an' illuminatin'.'

'I said it would only be a waste of time,' remarked Leek with great satisfaction. 'It's queer, but I get these hunches now an' again.'

'You only get a hunch that it's a waste of time when you have ter do somethin',' snapped Mr. Budd, rolling down his shirt sleeves and reaching for his coat. 'It won't hurt you to earn yer salary for a change.'

'I'm not grumblin',' protested the sergeant untruthfully. 'I don't mind what I do, so long as I get results.'

'The trouble is that whatever you do, there never *are* any results,' broke in his superior, putting on his jacket with difficulty and beginning to brush his hair. 'You're too impatient, that's what's the matter. You expect everythin' to 'appen at once.'

'What d'you think's goin' ter 'appen?'

126

demanded Leek.

Mr. Budd was so taken aback by the question that it was several seconds before he replied. 'Hm, well I don't rightly know, I s'pose. But I think somethin's goin' to happen, an' soon. Somethin's *got* to happen. Spooky Withers, Snodland, and Mrs. Claydon are up to somethin', an' sooner or later they'll do somethin' that'll tell us what it is. So you just get on with your job an' don't grouse.'

He went down in search of tea and found Peter Walton in the coffee-room, munching toast and jam. 'Hello, hello!' greeted the reporter. 'I thought the fairies had spirited you away. Where have you been?'

'Busy,' said Mr. Budd shortly.

'In other words, mind my own business,' said Peter with a grimace. 'You ought to know better than to expect any reporter to do that. What have you got up your sleeve?'

'Now look here, Walton,' said Mr. Budd severely, 'when I've got anythin' for you I'll tell you, an' not before.' He looked round. 'I should like some tea, if there's anyone to get it.'

'The fair damsel who waits upon us has gone to get me some cake,' said Peter. 'She ought to be back directly. Seriously, Budd, what do you think — '

'I don't,' said the superintendent warily. 'I've given up thinkin'. Ah, here she comes at last.'

One of Mr. Jephcott's numerous offspring appeared with a plate of cake and a beaming smile, took his order for tea, and departed.

'Do you mean to tell me that you're stumped?' inquired Peter, eyeing the cake approvingly.

'I don't mean to tell you anythin',' replied Mr. Budd, leaning back in his chair and yawning.

'Well, we're both in the same boat,' confessed the reporter ruefully. 'I can't find anything that makes sense in this murder.'

'The only thing that makes sense is that the victim was a reporter. It was a hell of a good precedent.' He got to his feet and moved towards the door.

'Here,' called Peter, twisting round in his chair. 'Where are you going?'

'I'm goin' to get them to send me tea up to me room,' grunted Mr. Budd, 'where I can 'ave it without 'avin' to listen to your silly chatter.'

He went out, leaving the reporter to finish his tea alone. Peter took a piece of cake and stared at it thoughtfully. His face had gone serious and his eyes were grave. He had a sudden queer feeling of impending tragedy — a vague chill that crept like stealthy fingers up his spine. There was no cause for it, and it was gone almost at once, but it left him anxious and troubled in mind.

12

The Light in the Night

With the setting of the sun, the weather changed. Great heavy black clouds, like billows of smoke, came rolling up from the west, and the wind freshened. By nine o'clock it was blowing a gale and pouring with rain.

Mr. Budd, sitting in a corner of the almost deserted bar at The Monk's Head, with a tankard of beer in front of him and one of his black cigars clamped in the corner of his mouth, listened to the wail of the wind and the hiss and splash of the rain and felt thankful that there was nothing to call him out on such a night.

Peter Walton, sitting in his room upstairs, tapped busily away at his battered typewriter, and found the noise of the storm blending with the click of the keys and producing a soothing effect that was rather pleasant.

The unfortunate Sergeant Leek, shivering in an old raincoat under the inadequate shelter of a clump of trees, silently cursed the weather and stared enviously at the dimly lighted windows of Abbot's Rest, his imagination picturing the warmth and comfort within and contrasting it, with a great deal of bitterness and self-pity, with his own wet, cold and unhappy environment.

At Abbotsway the trees bent and creaked before the heavy blasts of wind, and the old house shook and emitted strange noises — thuds and rattles and groans, as though an army of disembodied spirits had taken possession of it and were holding high revel.

Mrs. Shannon, knitting in a big chair by the fire in the drawing-room, started and looked up uneasily as each fresh gust of wind buffeted the old building and drove the rain violently against the window-panes. Her husband had fallen asleep over his book in the chair opposite her, and Michael was slumped in a corner of the settee reading. Eileen had gone to bed almost directly after dinner. Mrs.

Shannon was a little worried about her daughter. She had grown so listless lately, and easily tired. But the doctor had assured her soothingly, in reply to her agitated questions, that there was nothing physically the matter with Eileen. All the same, she was not entirely reassured. Doctors had been wrong before — look at that stupid man in India who had refused to believe that there was anything the matter with Mrs. Colington until she was dead — and there was definitely *something* the matter with Eileen. She hadn't been the same person at all recently, so nervous and strange and always looking as if she didn't get enough sleep . . .

A strange and appalling noise made her jump violently and drop her knitting. Michael looked up from his book and grinned. 'It's all right,' he murmured. 'Only Father snoring.'

The sound, like the death rattle of an expiring hippopotamus, rose in a terrifying crescendo and wavered in full cry; and, with a coughing gasp, Colonel Shannon woke up. The book that had been resting on his knee slid off and fell with a thud on the carpet.

'Ah, h-r-r-r-m!' He sat up and yawned. 'Must have dropped off for a minute. What's the time?'

'Nearly ten o'clock,' said Michael, glancing at the clock on the mantelpiece. As if in confirmation, the clock in the hall chimed the quarters and then struck the hour.

Colonel Shannon got up, stretched himself, picked up his book, put it on the small table beside his chair, and, going over to the fireplace, stood with his back to the fire. 'Beastly night,' he remarked, teetering slowly back and forth. 'Hark at the rain.'

Mrs. Shannon carefully folded up her knitting and deposited it in an embroidered bag she kept for this purpose. 'I think I shall go to bed, dear,' she said, rising and brushing down her dress.

'I shan't be long,' said her husband. 'You'd better go too, Michael. High time.'

Michael had no desire to go to bed. He would have preferred to remain where he was by the fire and finish his book, but experience warned him of the futility of arguing with the colonel. It would only lead to a lecture on the subject of discipline and the necessity of obedience. Colonel Shannon had never quite realized that his children were growing up and might have wishes of their own.

Even if he had, it is doubtful if it would have made very much difference. His long military career had convinced him that the only correct method of living was the method of the army. Even his wife had to submit to a rigid timetable that could only be deviated from in the case of illness. Colonel Shannon would have lived by numbers if it had been possible, and very nearly did.

After Michael had kissed his mother, said good night to his father, and gone to resume the reading of his book in bed, Bream came in with a tray. It was the colonel's invariable custom to take a nightcap before retiring, over which he smoked a final cigar. The nightcap consisted of three fingers of Haig whisky — he refused to drink any other brand — and a small splash of soda. This was brought in at ten o'clock precisely; and when he had finished it and his cigar, he went to bed.

'Three minutes late, Bream,' he grunted as the butler set down the tray.

'Yes, sir, I'm sorry,' said Bream. 'I had some trouble in fastening the scullery window, sir. It blew open earlier in the evening and the hinges were slightly strained.'

The colonel accepted the explanation with a nod. 'Better make sure that everything's securely fastened tonight. Nasty gale.'

'Yes, sir,' said Bream. He inquired as he always did if there was anything else, and, wishing his master and mistress good night, withdrew.

Colonel Shannon poured out his usual amount of whisky, added a splash of soda from the siphon, and held the glass up to the light. Then, seeing that his wife was still hovering about, he raised his eyebrows. 'Aren't you going to bed, m'dear?' he asked.

Mrs. Shannon gathered up her belongings and moved reluctantly towards the door. 'Yes . . . Yes, I'm going now, James,' she said. She had wanted to talk to him about Eileen and something else that was bothering her, but her desire was not strong enough to overcome her habitual nervousness about doing or saying anything that might incur his displeasure. And what she wanted to say would, she knew, most certainly meet with the strongest disapproval.

'Good night, m'dear,' said Colonel Shannon, opening the box of cigars on the small table and selecting one with care.

'Good night, James.'

She opened the door and went out into the big hall. The wind seemed to have increased in violence, and she could hear the beat of the rain on the shrubbery outside. Amid all that noise it would be difficult to sleep, she thought. She went slowly up the staircase, her shadow, thrown by the shaded light from below, sprawling and distorted on the wall behind her. This was the time she dreaded — this period between darkness and the coming of morning when she would lie in her bed wakeful and terrified, listening to every sound that reached her from the sleeping house. And sometimes she heard strange sounds — sounds that to her imagination were like stealthy steps creeping up the stairs and along the passage; sounds that were like the soft closing of doors and the brush of garments against panelling; sounds that she was convinced were made by nothing human.

For Mrs. Shannon was a great believer in the supernatural, and it was her firm opinion that Abbotsway was haunted, and that the legend of the Abbot of Felsbank was something more than an old wives' tale. The fact that she was forced to keep her fears to herself only added to her uneasiness and terror. But she knew that if she had breathed a word of her conviction to her husband, he would have been very angry indeed — so angry that she preferred to suffer in silence than risk it. She knew that she would receive no sympathy from him, only a lengthy lecture concerning the stupidity of allowing her nerves to get the better of her and the suggestion that she should overcome such childish nonsense. But although there was no practical foundation for them, her fears were, to her, very real and tangible things, and since the night of the murder and the burglary had increased immeasurably. Had she been her own mistress, she would have packed her things and fled from Abbotsway for good, thankful to be free from a house that she both feared and hated.

Outside the door of Eileen's room she paused and listened. The wind had lulled momentarily, and only the hiss of the falling rain broke the silence. Turning the handle, Mrs. Shannon pushed the door open an inch or two and peered in.

The room was in darkness and she caught the faint sound of steady breathing. Eileen must have gone to sleep already. Thankfully and a little enviously, she softly shut the door and made her way to her own room. As she entered it and switched on the light, a heavy gust of wind shook the house and rattled the window. She shut the door quickly and turned the key — she never slept with her door unlocked — and going over to the window, looked out through the rain-blurred panes. It was black as velvet outside and she could see nothing at all. Somewhere in that noisy blackness, beyond the garden and the wall and the old riverbed, lay the ruins of the abbey where a man had been bloodily done to death.

Mrs. Shannon shivered, hastily drew the curtains, and began to undress quickly. She pulled on a dressing-gown, unlocked the door, and tiptoed to the bathroom, glancing uneasily over her shoulder as she negotiated the long passage. When she had washed and brushed her teeth, she returned to her bedroom, relocked the door and got into bed.

The noise outside had not abated. The wind came surging across the open country, gathering force as it came, to hurl its strength, with the regularity of waves breaking on a beach, against the house, and the rain spattered on the window like the tapping of a thousand fingers.

Mrs. Shannon, with the light beside her

bed still on, lay and stared at the ceiling, as wakeful as though it were midday and wishing fervently that it was. After what seemed an eternity she heard her husband come up and enter his room. For some little while afterward, she could hear him moving about; and then, with the exception of the usual queer creaks and rustlings, there was silence within the house.

Exactly when she dropped into a fitful doze she was uncertain — it must have been a long time after she came to bed — but whenever it was, she woke from it suddenly with a start, her heart beating violently and an icy chill of fear prickling her spine. The tumult outside had died down to a low murmur and there was no sound at all from within. What had caused her to start from that uneasy sleep to this frightened wakefulness? Something that had percolated to her brain through the mists of sleep?

She sat up in bed listening intently, her eyes turning suddenly first to the door and then to the curtained window. But she could hear nothing — find no cause for the terror that still shook her. Perhaps it was something she had dreamed — and yet she could recollect nothing; was not conscious of any dream. But *something* must have wakened her — *something* must have caused this dread that filled her soul and made her body shiver as though she had an ague.

Obeying an impulse she would have found difficult to explain, she got out of bed, went to the window, and pulled aside the curtains. The night was still pitch black, and somewhere far away the wind still moaned, but it appeared to have stopped raining. And then she caught her breath as if she had suddenly been plunged into ice-cold water. A light had glimmered in the darkness — a pinpoint of radiance that moved like a gigantic firefly back and forth and back again. And it came from the ancient ruins of Felsbank Abbey.

13

Missing!

It was Colonel Shannon's boast that, although he slept soundly, he was capable of waking at an instant's notice in complete possession of all his senses. That this was an exaggeration of which his wife was fully aware, and had the fact further demonstrated when she shook him by the shoulder. He grunted, gasped, twisted petulantly on to his back and opened one eye.

'Wasamarra?' he demanded huskily. 'Whatisit?'

'Wake up,' said Mrs. Shannon in an agitated whisper. 'Please wake up, James. There's somebody in the ruins. I saw a light . . . '

'All right,' grunted the colonel. Closing his eye, he turned over on his other side with great determination and promptly went to sleep again.

'James! Please listen to me.' His wife shook him once more. 'Please wake up, James!'

'What the hell's th'matter?' This time the colonel opened both eyes and blinked resentfully at her. 'What is it? What do you want?'

She explained hurriedly and succeeded in penetrating his sleep-drugged brain.

'Somebody in the ruins . . . light . . . ?' He sat up and rubbed his head. 'Begad! What's it to do with me?'

'Oh, don't you see?' Excitement and fear had rendered Mrs. Shannon almost incoherent. 'Something dreadful may be happening there!'

'Nonsense! Rubbish!' said the colonel testily. He was rapidly becoming wide awake and feeling cross at this disturbance of his slumbers. 'You've been dreaming. Go back to bed.'

'I wasn't dreaming,' asserted his wife tearfully. 'There was a light in the ruins. I saw it from my window!'

'If there were fifty thousand candle-power arcs, it's got nothing to do with me!' declared Colonel Shannon. 'Damnit, why should I bother about it? If some lunatic likes to spend his time wandering about the blasted place, it's no concern of mine.'

'The same thing may be happening again,' whimpered Mrs. Shannon. 'I'm sure somebody's going to be murdered.'

Her husband looked at her as though he was quite prepared to believe it, and could offer more than a suggestion concerning the victim. And then an idea apparently occurred to him, for his eyes glinted, and he suddenly swung himself out of bed and went over to the window. Jerking the curtains aside, he peered out.

'I can't see anything,' he muttered. 'It's as dark as the pit.'

'It was there. A tiny light — like a torch. It kept shifting backwards and forwards.'

'Begad, you're right,' snapped the colonel suddenly, and a note of excitement crept into his voice. 'There *is* a light, and it's moving about — looks as if somebody's searching for something.' He turned quickly away from the window and began to scramble hurriedly into his clothes.

'What are you going to do?' enquired

his wife anxiously.

'See what's going on. Catch this prowler, whoever it is, and find out what he's doing.'

'Oh, do be careful. It may be dangerous!'

'Dangerous? Rubbish!' retorted the colonel, struggling into a tweed jacket. 'Remember that time I went through the enemy's lines in Burma? Begad, *that* was dangerous.'

Mrs. Shannon, who had heard the story of this gallant deed so often that she knew it by heart, interrupted: 'But this is different!'

'Different?' exclaimed her husband, unlocking a drawer and producing an enormous old-fashioned service revolver the size of a young cannon. 'Of course it's different — child's play. Now you go back to bed and don't worry.'

Mrs. Shannon had no intention of going back to bed or of refraining from worrying, but custom prevented her from arguing, and she followed her husband out into the passage and along to the head of the staircase. But she remained while he carefully descended to the hall and opened the front door. It was still very dark outside, but not quite as dark as it had been. The rain had ceased and the wind had dropped slightly, although it was still fairly strong, and one or two stars were visible between the gaps in the clouds. The weather was clearing.

Colonel Shannon closed the front door gently behind him and struck out across the soggy lawn towards the gate in the yew hedge, the big revolver clutched tightly in his right hand. From this lower level it was impossible to see anything of the ruins; and the wind, whistling round him, effectually drowned any sound there might have been. If, however, the owner of the light was still there, the colonel was determined to find out who it was and what they were doing.

It would give him great pleasure to take that fat detective from Scotland Yard down a peg or two. Make him realize that an army man could show him a few points, what! It was the prospect of this that had made him decide on his course of action. With a sense of adventure he had not experienced for many a long day, Colonel Shannon squelched his way forward. He reached the gate, which unlike the Abbot's Gate in the other wall was never fastened, opened it, and came out onto the strip of road.

Out of the shelter of the garden the wind was stiffer, but the darkness seemed less. He could see, across the dip of the old riverbed, the ruins of the abbey loom up, an irregular dark blot against the almost equally dark sky.

He paused, searching for some sign that there was anyone lurking in the ancient pile. But he could see nothing, nor hear any sound. The light was no longer visible. The gloomy place looked completely deserted.

Colonel Shannon moved forward stealthily. Truth be told, he was thoroughly enjoying, himself. This stalking of a possible enemy in the darkness of the night carried him back to his old campaigning days and made him feel curiously younger. A tinge of the old excitement coursed through his veins and stirred to life something that had long lain dormant.

He came up the slope at the foot of the ruins and stopped under cover of a broken wall to listen. It was a tribute to his fitness that his breathing was as steady and even as if he had been sitting in his own drawing-room.

There was no sound except the rush of the wind and the drip, drip of water. He crept along by the side of the wall, came to an opening, and a moment later was inside the ruins. No light now or movement. Whoever had been there was either crouching silently in one of the many hiding-places the abbey offered or had gone.

The colonel hesitated. It would be difficult to make a thorough search of the ruins in the dark, and he had forgotten to provide himself with a torch. All the same, he was loath to leave before satisfying himself that there was no one there. Either his eyes were growing accustomed to the darkness, or it was getting lighter.

He looked up at the sky and saw that it was the latter. The driving clouds were thinning rapidly, and behind the racing wrack the ghost of a dim moon was visible. Soon there would be light enough to make an examination of the place possible.

He moved forward over the grass-grown paving, carefully negotiating the heaps of wet stones, and passed under the broken arch. The truncated tower and what was left of the cloisters lay before him, but there was no sign of human presence other than his own.

The moon came out, shining clearly, and turning the whole place into a scene of silver and black — of vivid highlights and dense shadows. Before it disappeared again, the colonel made a quick but thorough search. Nobody. But there had *been* somebody. There was a confused jumble of fresh footprints in the mud, and a trail that led back across the open space to a gap.

Colonel Shannon frowned. Why should anyone have come to the ruins in the middle of such a stormy night? Could it have been some tramp seeking shelter from the wind and rain? Surely in that case he would be there still. Or perhaps, when the rain had ceased, he had gone upon his way. It was a possible explanation, but not a very satisfying one.

The colonel left the ruins, disappointed with the uneventful ending to his expedition. The momentary flood of moonlight had vanished, and when he reached his own gate he came upon the figure of his wife with such startling suddenness that it gave him a shock. She wore a dressing-gown over her nightdress and had thrust her feet into slippers.

'What are you doing here?' demanded the colonel a little harshly. 'You'll catch your death of cold.'

'Is she with you?' asked Mrs. Shannon breathlessly.

'Who?' snapped the colonel testily.

'Eileen.' His wife's voice rose sharply. 'Then where is she?'

'Isn't she in bed?'

'No,' wailed Mrs. Shannon, 'no. She's not in bed, and she's not in the house. She's gone . . . gone . . . gone . . . ' She began to sob wildly and uncontrollably.

14

The Letter

Mr. Budd, sleepy-eyed and frowning, stood in the drawing-room at Abbotsway and gently rubbed the lowest of his many chins. The chill of dawn was in the air and a cold grey light filtered in through the window, making the electric lamps look curiously garish. Colonel Shannon, dishevelled and haggard, stood in front of the dead fire, while Mrs. Shannon, red-eyed and looking on the point of collapse, huddled in a chair. Peter Walton, with his back to the room, stared silently out of the window at the unpromising beginning of the day.

The urgent ringing of the telephone in the small hours of that morning had awakened Mr. Jephcott from his just sleep, who, in turn, had wakened Mr. Budd, and over the wire that yawning man had heard the incoherent and almost unrecognizable voice of Colonel Shannon telling him of the latest development in the Monk's Ferry mystery.

He had agreed to come to Abbotsway at once, and was getting out his car when Peter Walton, apparently awakened by the ringing of the telephone too, had put in an appearance and demanded to be told what was going on. Realizing that he would be bound to hear sooner or later, the superintendent told him, and Peter had pleaded to be allowed to come along.

They had reached Abbotsway just as the sky was paling in the east, and heard in detail the story of the night and its culmination. Mr. Budd had been a trifle sceptical at first, concluding that very probably Eileen Shannon had gone somewhere for reasons of her own; but an examination of her bedroom had quickly made him change his opinion.

The bed had been slept in and was tumbled and untidy. The window was open, and ranged against the sill was a light ladder which, the colonel asserted, was used by the gardener and always kept at the back of the house. More significant than anything was the discovery of a large pad of cotton wool, still reeking of chloroform, which the superintendent found near the foot of the ladder in a flowerbed.

Here, too, he discovered a number of confused footprints from which two tracks led away across the lawn to the gate giving onto the road, while another track was traceable round to the place where the ladder had been kept. The prints had been made by two people, both men from the size of them, and it was fairly easy to reconstruct what had happened.

The ladder had been fetched and put up, and one of the men had ascended to the window while the other waited below. Eileen always slept with the casement open an inch or two, and secured by an iron bar in which were regular holes that fitted into a stud in the wooden frame; and in spite of the inclemency of the night had evidently adhered to her usual custom. This had made it easy for the intruder, who had only to insert something that would lift the bar from its stud to open the window and effect an entrance. The noises of the stormy night would have drowned the slight sound that would have been made, and before she could have become aware of what was happening and given the alarm, the chloroform pad could have been pressed over her face and in a few seconds she would have succumbed to the drug.

The man waiting below, at a signal from the other, could then have mounted the ladder, received the unconscious woman and carried her down, the other man following. It would have taken barely ten minutes to carry out the whole plan. Mr. Budd formulated the theory of what had happened from the various traces the men concerned had been forced to leave behind, and was pretty certain that it was roughly correct. An old tweed suit of Eileen's was missing from the wardrobe, and it seemed likely that they had either dressed her in it or taken it to dress her later.

The detective was inclined to think the latter. The question was, where had she been taken, and why? An examination of the footprints' tracks had shown that they came and went to the ruins, but from thence there was no sign. The ground was so churned up in the vicinity that it was impossible to trace them further. There was an impression of tyres further along the road where a car had evidently waited, but they were not very clear. The question of 'where' was therefore for the present unanswerable, but the question of 'why' was altogether a different matter. Mr. Budd thought there was very little difficulty in finding a reason for the woman's abduction, and put his opinion into words in reply to Colonel Shannon's frantic question.

'I think she knew somethin' concernin' the murder of Lloyd Gibbs, sir,' he said ponderously. 'Somethin' that threatened the murderer's safety.'

'Knew something — about the murder?' The colonel gaped at him. 'What *could* she have known?

'I can't tell you that, but I'm sure she wasn't tellin' the truth about that night. I never have thought she was tellin' the truth. Part of it, p'r'aps, but not all of it.'

'I don't understand you, sir,' said Colonel Shannon stiffly. 'Are you insinuating that my daughter is a liar?'

'Well yes, sir, I s'pose I am,' agreed Mr. Budd. 'It's my belief that when your daughter stated she didn't look out of her window that night when she heard the scream, she was lyin'. I believe she *did* look out of her window, an' she saw somethin', an' that it's because of what she saw that this has happened.'

'But why should she lie?' demanded the colonel.

'I'd like ter know that too, sir.' Mr. Budd shrugged. 'I've been wonderin' that for a long time.'

'There's no sense in your suggestion,' declared Colonel Shannon emphatically. 'If my daughter had seen anything, she would have said so. There's no reason why she shouldn't.'

'There wouldn't appear to be,' murmured Mr. Budd doubtfully, 'but I think there was.'

'What you are suggesting,' snapped the colonel angrily, 'is that my daughter was in some way mixed up in this murder! It's ridiculous and absurd.'

'Oh, can't you do anything except stand there arguing?' broke in Mrs.

156

Shannon impatiently. 'Don't you realize that Eileen's gone — that she may be dead — that . . . '

'I don't think you need fear *that*,' said Peter, turning suddenly from the window and his silent inspection of the garden. 'If these people had any intention of killing your daughter, they would have killed her here. They wouldn't have gone to all the trouble and risk of taking her away.'

'There's somethin' in that, Walton,' agreed Mr. Budd, nodding.

'Which means that there's something more behind this abduction of Miss Shannon than that she saw or knew something that was dangerous to someone's safety,' continued the reporter. 'If it was only that, the easiest way to ensure her silence would have been to kill her on the spot, not take her away.'

'Can you suggest any reason why she should have been taken away?' inquired Mr. Budd, his sleepy eyes suddenly opening very wide.

'No, I can't,' answered Peter candidly. 'But I'm willing to bet that it's a pretty big one. These people aren't going to burden themselves with a woman whom all the police in the country will be looking for within a few hours, unless the reason justifies the risk. That's common sense.'

It was, and the detective admitted it.

'What does it matter *why* they took her?' cried Mrs. Shannon. 'All that matters is to find her and bing her back. Why don't you do something about that, instead of just talking?'

'We're doin' all we can, madam,' said Mr. Budd gently.

'What *are* you doing?' demanded Mrs. Shannon. 'You're just wasting time, that's all.'

'Come, m'dear,' interposed the colonel soothingly, 'try and control yourself. Why don't you go and lie down.'

'I don't want to lie down,' said Mrs. Shannon tearfully. 'I want Eileen.' She suddenly burst into a fit of sobbing. 'I wish I'd never come to this beastly house! I've always known that something dreadful would happen here. There's a curse on it! I've always felt there was, and I was right, though nobody would ever listen to me.'

'M'dear . . . ' remonstrated her husband, but she took no notice of him.

'This is a wicked, evil place, and the evil is not finished.' She stopped abruptly, raising her tear-stained face. 'What's that?' she asked sharply. The others had not heard the sound of the approaching car, but now that their attention was drawn to it, it was clearly audible.

'Superintendent Boyder,' said Mr. Budd, whose first action on reaching Abbotsway, after he had heard the news, had been to ring the police station at Barnford.

Boyder it was, unshaven and hastily dressed, and obviously very worried and puzzled. 'This is a shocking business,' he remarked when he had been told all they knew. 'Have you any reason to suspect anybody, sir?'

'Suspect anybody?' echoed the colonel. 'Whom should I suspect? Good God, man, I know nothing more than you do.'

'Well there must be a motive,' said Boyder. 'That's the first thing to look for.'

'The first thing to look for is my daughter,' broke in Mrs. Shannon, who had recovered herself a little. 'Reasons

— motives — what do they matter? My daughter is the only thing that matters.'

'Yes, yes, quite so, madam,' agreed the local superintendent hastily. 'But if we can find the motive, we shall be more than halfway towards discovering who's responsible for your daughter's disappearance.'

'Find the motive for the murder of Lloyd Gibbs,' murmured Mr. Budd, 'an' you'll find the motive for Miss Shannon's abduction.'

'You think the two are connected?' said Boyder.

'All these various things are part of one main thing,' said Mr. Budd with conviction. 'It's absurd to s'pose that a whole bunch of crooks have suddenly collected in Monk's Ferry to carry out distinct an' separate schemes of their own. You've *got* to believe that it's all one scheme. It don't make sense any other way.'

'It doesn't make sense any way to me,' grunted the bewildered superintendent. 'What can anyone want with Miss Shannon?'

Mr. Budd thought he might have

phrased it a little better, but realized what he meant. 'Why did anyone want to kill Gibbs?' he retorted. 'For what reason did someone dressed as a monk break into this house the other night? Find the answer to any one of those questions and you've found the answer to the lot.'

'In the meantime my daughter is probably being murdered,' cried Mrs. Shannon. 'Oh, do stop *talking* and *do* something.'

'Have you a photograph of Miss Shannon?' asked Peter.

Mr. Budd shot him a suspicious glance. 'Look here, Walton — if you're thinkin' of publishin' anythin' in that wretched rag o' yours . . . '

'I'm going to print the whole story with a photograph and a description of the missing woman,' interrupted Peter coolly. 'It can't do any harm, and it might do a great deal of good.'

'Yes, yes!' broke in Mrs. Shannon eagerly. 'I'll give you a photograph.' She got up and went over to a bureau and started rummaging in one of the drawers.

'I should like one, too, madam,' said Superintendent Boyder. 'It will be useful to the police in circulating a description of Miss Shannon.'

Mr. Budd said nothing. In his opinion, neither the efforts of a national newspaper nor the routine methods of the police were likely to prove very helpful in the finding of Eileen Shannon. The people who had gone to so much trouble to take her would be prepared for all the normal procedures. Still, as Peter had stated, it could do no harm.

'Here you are.' Mrs. Shannon came back with a big envelope. She handed it to Peter, and at that moment Bream came in with a tray of coffee.

'Excuse me, sir,' he said, approaching the colonel. 'I found this letter in the box.'

'Letter?' His master looked at the envelope lying on the tray and frowned. 'It's much too early for the post.'

'It didn't come by post, sir. It must have been put in the box by hand. There is no stamp on it, sir.'

Colonel Shannon took the envelope and slit it open. He withdrew the single sheet of paper it contained, and as he read what was written on it, Mr. Budd saw his face change.

'What is it?' said Mrs. Shannon, coming over to him quickly. 'Is it anything to do with Eileen?'

He folded the note hastily and thrust it into his pocket. 'No,' he answered. 'No. It's . . . it's only an account . . . from . . . from Sanders the newsagent.'

'But you paid him last week. Why has he sent another?'

'Made a mistake, I suppose,' grunted the colonel. 'Pour out the coffee, Bream.'

Mr. Budd accepted the cup which the butler presently handed to him and gulped the hot coffee gratefully, but he was puzzled and curious. He was convinced the note had not come from Sanders the newsagent, or any other local tradesman, and he was certain that it was not an account. But why had Shannon lied? He would have given a great deal to know the real contents of the letter the colonel had so hurriedly concealed, and which had caused that queer expression of mingled astonishment, relief, and fear to come into his face as he read it.

15

Mr. Budd Receives a Visitor

The news of Eileen Shannon's abduction spread with the rapidity of a flood through the village, and by noon little groups of the inhabitants were discussing it in the narrow high street, in the small shops, and over the dividing fences of their gardens. It was seized upon with avidity as a subject of conversation, and there was much speculation and shaking of heads. A wave of superstitious fear, started by the murder and fed by this latest development, flowed over Monk's Ferry like a tidal wave, engulfing nearly everybody.

The fact that Mrs. Shannon had seen a strange light in the ruins of the abbey on the night of her daughter's disappearance was made much of. The old legend of the ghostly Abbot of Felsbank, never entirely discounted, was resuscitated and enlarged upon. People swore that they, too, had seen weird and inexplicable lights hovering in the vicinity of the ruins during the preceding weeks; and some, more imaginative, embellished their stories with tales of having heard the chanting of monks. Mrs. Shannon's mysterious light became unearthly fire playing around the figure of the abbot as he paced the ruins, wringing his hands and moaning in anguish. Only Mr. Jephcott and one or two of the more sensible residents adopted a practical viewpoint, and treated the general gossip with the scepticism it deserved.

Mr. Budd, called over to Barnford in the afternoon to attend a conference with the chief constable and Superintendent Boyder, had an interview with Sergeant Leek before he left. 'You're quite sure nobody left Abbot's Rest durin' the night?' he asked. 'You didn't fall asleep or somethin'?'

''Ave you ever known me neglect me duty?' Leek demanded in an injured tone. 'I never closed me eyes all night. An' what a night! There was rain blowin' in me face an' drippin' down me back . . . '

'An' you was standin' in a puddle an' yer boots was full o' water,' snarled Mr. Budd ill-temperedly. 'You've told me all that. What I want ter know is, did anybody leave the house?'

'No,' asserted the sergeant. 'They went to bed like sensible people — an' considerin' what sort of a night it was, I don't blame 'em!'

The superintendent made a gesture of disgust. He had hoped that Leek's report would involve the inhabitants of Abbot's Rest in Eileen Shannon's disappearance. 'What time did this feller from Barnford relieve you?' he asked, clutching at a last possible straw.

'At five o'clock this mornin',' answered Leek promptly, 'an' I was never more thankful ter see anybody. By that time I was so — '

'Wet they could've wrung you out like a soaked rag,' snapped Mr. Budd, ending his sentence for him. 'Though how you could be wetter than you are normally is more'n I can understand. Could you see both the front and the back of this place from where you were?'

'Yes,' said Leek with a resigned sigh, and he described the exact position he had taken up to watch the activities of the three inhabitants.

'Well,' said Mr. Budd, frowning, 'it seems pretty obvious *they* can't have had anything to do with this business. And if they didn't, who the devil did?'

'If you want my opinion . . . ' began the sergeant conversationally.

'I don't!' interrupted the detective rudely. 'This case is quite bad enough without you buttin' in with opinions.'

'I was only goin' ter make a suggestion,' protested the long-suffering Leek mournfully.

'Oh, all right, go ahead. Let's 'ear this brilliant suggestion.'

'It's this,' began Leek, and he rather diffidently explained.

Mr. Budd listened in silence until he had finished, and then he frowned and rubbed his massive chin. 'Hm,' he said slowly. 'There *might* be somethin' in that.'

'I think there's a lot in it,' said the gratified sergeant complacently. 'It took me a long time to work it out.'

'I'll turn it over in me mind,' said Mr. Budd thoughtfully. 'I believe you've hit on somethin'.'

'These things come to me,' said Leek, basking happily in this faint praise. 'They sort o' seep up out of the unconscious.'

'They couldn't seep out of anythin' else with you,' said Mr. Budd. 'It's the first idea you've 'ad for eighteen months, so it ought to be good. Now I must go an' see this blasted chief constable.'

The 'blasted chief constable' proved to be a dapper, wiry little man with very definite views of his own concerning the way the case was being handled, which he expressed more forcibly than politely. Mr. Budd spent a very trying two hours, during which he kept his temper with the greatest difficulty and listened to a vast amount of quite useless advice.

'Bit trying, isn't he?' remarked Superintendent Boyder wryly, when the conference was over.

'That's puttin' it very mildly,' said Mr. Budd.

He drove back to The Monk's Head,

where he was immediately accosted by Mr. Jephcott, who had apparently been on the lookout for him. 'Mr. Ashford wants to have a word with you, sir,' said the landlord. 'He's inside now.'

'Who's Mr. Ashford?'

'He's the owner of Long Meadow Farm. Lives there with his mother. Very nice young fellow.'

'What does he want to see me about?' inquired the superintendent as he got stiffly out of his car.

Mr. Jephcott could offer no suggestion about this. 'He's been waiting some time,' he said. 'He's in the coffee-room having a cup of tea.'

Mr. Budd put away his car and went expectantly into the coffee-room. Its only occupant was a pleasant-looking young man with a brown freckled face and a mop of rather unruly dark hair, who was staring at an empty tea-cup.

'You wanted to see me, sir?' inquired Mr. Budd, going over and sitting down in front of the visitor.

'If you are Superintendent Budd, yes,' was the reply.

'That's me. What can I do for you, sir?'

The young man's face was drawn and there was a strained look about his eyes. 'Have you — have you any news about Miss Shannon?'

Mr. Budd looked at him for a moment in interested silence, then slowly shook his head. 'No, sir, no news at all. But we're doin' everythin' that's possible. May I ask why you're so interested?'

'Miss Shannon is a friend of mine,' said Ashford. 'I'm naturally rather anxious to know what's being done to find her.'

'A friend of the family, are you?'

'Well . . . ' The young man hesitated. 'Well, not exactly. No, I can't say that . . . '

'A friend of Miss Shannon's, but not a friend of the family,' murmured Mr. Budd, and he nodded. 'I think I understand, sir.'

'Do you?' Ashford looked at him sharply, met the superintendent's sympathetic and benevolent eye, and smiled faintly. 'Well, yes, perhaps you do, partly.'

'Rather a — er — difficult gentleman, Colonel Shannon,' remarked Mr. Budd thoughtfully.

'A pig-headed old martinet!' declared

Ashford with feeling.

Mr. Budd's eyes twinkled. It was rather the way he would have described the colonel himself. 'How long have you been a — friend of Miss Shannon's?' he asked.

'About two years.' Ashford fiddled with the spoon in his saucer. 'You see, I've lived here all my life — at Long Meadow. By the way, I'd better introduce myself. My name's Gordon Ashford — I'd seen Eileen about the village, and I rather liked the look of her. One day I summoned up enough courage to speak to her. We got friendly, and I asked her to marry me. She said yes, but old Shannon wasn't having any of *that*. He kicked up the devil of a shine — forbade Eileen to speak to me and all the rest of it, like something out of a play or a book. We became secretly engaged, and she used to meet me whenever she got a chance — which wasn't often, because the old chap used to keep a pretty strict eye on her. I'm telling you this so that you'll know why I'm so worried about her disappearance.'

'I see,' murmured Mr. Budd, who had expected something of this sort. 'Well, I can understand you bein' worried, Mr. Ashford. I don't mind admittin' that I'm worried myself.'

'What do you think has happened to her?'

'To be perfectly candid, I don't know,' said Mr. Budd frankly. 'I'll tell you my opinion, but I don't think it's goin' to help much.' He repeated what he had said to the colonel that morning.

Gordon Ashford listened with knitted brows. 'But why, if she saw something, didn't she say what she saw?' he demanded when the superintendent had finished.

'That's what I'd like to know. I don't know why she should lie about it, but I'm quite sure she did.'

'I can understand why they should want to keep her quiet if she knew something,' muttered Gordon, 'but not why they should take her away. It would've been easier . . . ' He left the sentence unfinished, but Mr. Budd knew what he meant.

'That's one o' the things that puzzles me too,' he said. 'Maybe there's somethin' more at the back of it than what I think. I hope there is.'

'It would mean that she — that she would be safer?' said Gordon quickly.

The detective nodded. 'Yes, sir. Not that I think she's come to any harm,' he added hastily. 'She wouldn't have been taken away if they'd meant to — hurt her.'

'There's no clue, no trace?'

'None whatever. Of course, there's no sayin' but when there will be. Every policeman in the country's on the lookout, an' we may get news at any moment.'

'Will you let me know at once, if you do?' asked Gordon. 'And if there's anything I can do to help . . . '

Mr. Budd promised. He liked this young man who was trying so hard to be matter-of-fact in his grief and anxiety. 'If you've lived 'ere so long,' he said, 'you must know pretty well everybody in the place?'

'Most of them, anyway.'

'Did you know Marie?' inquired Mr. Budd casually.

'Everitt Marie — the man who was arrested, and lived at Abbotsway before the Shannons?' Gordon nodded. 'I knew him rather well. I used to supply him with a lot of farm produce. He was interested in farming and we used to have long talks. I liked him.'

'Did he ever say anythin' about the history of the place?'

'Yes, he was very interested in that, too. Particularly the history of Felsbank Abbey and the story of the Twelve Apostles — you've heard about that, I suppose?'

'Yes, I've 'eard about that,' assented Mr. Budd. 'Marie was interested in that, was he?'

'Look here,' said Gordon, eyeing him searchingly, 'what are you getting at? Marie's dead, isn't he? I thought I read in the papers that he'd died in prison.'

'You did. Everitt Marie's dead — an' so is Stephenson, the feller who discovered the steam engine, but there are still railway trains runnin' all over the world.'

'Meaning what?' Gordon asked, puzzled.

'When a man's dead,' said Mr. Budd gently, 'his activities don't always die, too. Tell me, Mr. Ashford, did Marie ever say anythin' to you about a key?'

16

The Story of the Key

Gordon Ashford stared at the superintendent with an expression of bewilderment that was almost ludicrous.

'How in the world did you know anything about that?' he demanded at length. 'I'd forgotten all about it myself.'

Mr. Budd yawned, partly to conceal the excitement that surged suddenly up inside him. 'So he *did* say somethin' about a key,' he murmured softly.

'No, he didn't. He *found* a key, which is a different matter. I was with him when it happened.'

'Tell me about it,' asked Mr. Budd eagerly.

'That's all very well, but aren't you rather wasting time? The most important thing at the moment is to try and find Eileen.'

'Look here, Mr. Ashford,' broke in the

detective, 'a few seconds ago you said you wanted to help, an' now that I'm askin' you to, you're quibblin'.'

'But I don't see how this could help.'

'Maybe you don't, an' I'm not goin' to tell you how — not yet, anyway — but it's goin' to help a lot. You can take my word for that.'

'Oh, well . . . ' Gordon shrugged resignedly. 'I suppose you know more about it than I do. It won't take very long to tell, anyhow. The dog that now belongs to that appalling little squirt, Snodland, used to belong to Marie — '

'Bisto?' interjected Mr. Budd.

Gordon nodded. 'Dreadful name, isn't it? But a jolly nice dog all the same. As I say, he used to belong to Marie — Snodland bought him when Marie was arrested — and whenever Marie came over to see me, Bisto came with him. He was very fond of the dog, and used to take it with him everywhere. One day Marie had been over to the farm, and I walked back with him — I forget what I came back for; it doesn't matter — and Bisto, as usual, was scampering ahead of

176

us, nosing into everything that took his fancy. We were following the course of the old riverbed, and the dog had gone racing ahead of us and we lost sight of him.

'We heard him barking excitedly in the distance, but we didn't take much notice. Then, as we caught up with him, we saw that he was digging furiously in a patch of ground near the ruins, growling and whimpering with delight. Marie called him, but he only paused for a moment to look up impatiently and then continued his labours. 'I wonder what he's found?' said Marie, and we went over to look.

'Bisto had dug a pretty fair-sized hole — it had been raining heavily during the morning and the ground was soft — and his muzzle and paws were covered with mud. He wagged his tail and broke into a crescendo of barking as we inspected his handiwork, and then began to worry at something in the hole. It looked like a bit of rusty iron, and that's what it was, as we found when we succeeded in pulling it out — a big iron key, rusty and corroded. It was a massive affair, the sort of key that might have unlocked the main door of the abbey. Marie said it was probably the Abbot's Key, and put it in his pocket as a curiosity, much to the disgust of Bisto, who had done all the work in finding it and quite obviously thought he should have the prize. That was the last time I saw Marie. Two days later he was arrested.'

Mr. Budd's expression was calm and rather bored. No one could have guessed at the excitement that seethed within him. The Abbot's Key! The words that Lew Cator had muttered before he died. And Marie had found it. Here was a fresh piece of the puzzle to be fitted into place. 'D'you know what happened to this key?' he asked.

'No; I'd forgotten all about it until now. I suppose it was sold with the rest of the stuff to Colonel Shannon.'

'He's never even heard of it,' murmured Mr. Budd. 'That is, if he's speakin' the truth. But somebody else has heard of it — somebody who wanted it so badly that they broke into Abbotsway to try an' get it.'

'Do you mean *that* was the reason for

the burglary?' demanded Gordon in astonishment. 'But — '

'That's what *I* think. But remember, I 'aven't any proof ter go on.'

'But why should anybody want the key? It's valueless except as a curiosity. And how did they know anything about it?'

'Look here, Mr. Ashford,' Mr. Budd said deliberately, 'I've got an idea that I can trust you. An' I don't mind admittin' that I can do with the help of somebody round here who knows the place an' whom I can trust.'

'You *can* trust me,' interposed Gordon quickly. 'I'll do anything I can to help.'

'Then you've got to promise that whatever I tell you won't go any further. The safety of Miss Shannon may depend on it, so I'm warnin' you.'

'I promise,' declared Ashford. 'I won't say a word.'

'You asked me if I'd heard the story of the silver Twelve Apostles,' said Mr. Budd, glancing quickly round and lowering his voice, 'an' I told you I had. Well, I think them things is at the bottom of all this queer business.'

'But people have been looking for them for years. Some time ago, several well-known archaeologists spent nearly eighteen months in the district searching.'

'But they didn't know where to look, an' where they looked was in the wrong places. I think Everitt Marie was luckier. I think he *did* know where to look, an' I think he would have found 'em if he hadn't been arrested before he had time. I think that key he found an' called the Abbot's Key held the secret — the place where the old abbot hid them statues.'

'But even if you're right,' said Gordon, 'Marie's dead.'

'Yes, he's dead. He died in Wormwood Scrubs last October. But that don't say that before he died he didn't pass on what he knew to *someone else*.'

'Who?'

'Ah yes, that's what I don't know. Who? The person who killed Gibbs an' broke into Abbotsway an' abducted Miss Shannon. A feller who at one time called himself Jackson, I think, but is probably callin' himself somethin' different now. A feller who's after a million quid in solid silver an' isn't goin' to let anythin' stop him gettin' it. But who? That's somethin' I'm very anxious to know, Mr. Ashford — very anxious indeed.'

*   *   *

Colonel Shannon, sitting alone in his bedroom, read the letter he had received that morning for the twentieth time, although he already knew the contents by heart.

Your daughter is safe and will continue to remain so, provided that you will agree to a small request. Come alone to the Abbot's Gate at twelve tonight and you will hear more. Keep the contents of this note to yourself or you will never see your daughter again.

There was no signature, no address, nothing more at all, and the letter had been typewritten. Colonel Shannon pulled at his moustache and glanced at the clock on the bedside table. It was quarter past eleven. In three quarters of an hour he would be at the gate and find out what this queer epistle was all about.

He had very nearly told the police about it when Bream had brought it in, but the threat in it had stopped him. It could do no harm to keep the appointment, and it might do a lot of good. He supposed it was money they were after. Well, he hadn't a lot, but he was prepared to go a very long way to get his daughter back safe and sound. In spite of his sternness and despotic method of ruling his family, he was very fond of them. He had been brought up in the same strict way, and he thought it was a good way. The rod had not been spared, and it was impossible for him to believe that he had been spoiled.

He had not mentioned the letter to his wife. Time enough for that if anything came of it. He was not a believer in raising hopes that might end in disappointment, although Mrs. Shannon was almost beside herself with grief and worry. He had thought of confiding in Michael, but had decided against it almost before the thought had formed. He was not accustomed to confiding in anybody, preferring to work things out on his own. He had always had to.

That the disappearance of his daughter had affected him deeply was evident in the added lines between his eyes and a drawn, tense look about his whole face, but he was a stoic and did not believe in giving way to outward emotion. This stern suppressing of his feelings made his sufferings all the more acute since there was no safety valve to give relief, and in consequence he probably felt a great deal more deeply than Mrs. Shannon.

The house, except for its usual queer creakings, was very quiet as he waited for the time to pass. Outside was a clear sky and moonlight. Well, so much the better. He would be able to see the writer of the letter distinctly. It must have been put in the box during the night of Eileen's abduction — probably directly after she had been taken away. No doubt they had it all ready. Where was she?

It was a relief to know that she was safe, at any rate; and it was a good thing that this negotiation had not to be left to that fat, sleepy-looking fool from Scotland Yard. A pretty sort of detective *he* was, with his impertinent and absurd idea that Eileen knew anything about the murder of this newspaper reporter, and accusing her of lying! He would have a pretty stiff word to say about that to the chief commissioner when all this was over. These fellows got too big for their boots. Not used to dealing with respectable people of his class, that was the size of it. He'd show them that they couldn't insult members of *his* family with impunity.

The country was going to the dogs. He could remember when people treated you with respect. It was the same with the tradespeople. At one time they had been glad enough to get your custom, and, having got it, they went to some trouble to keep it. But now they seemed to imagine that they were conferring a favour on you by serving you at all. It was all damned wrong, this business of equality. The army knew better than that. Respect for position and discipline — that was what was wanted in civil life.

It wouldn't be long now before he would discover just what was at the back of that letter. 'A small request . . . ' How much would it be? If it was within his power, he was prepared to agree, whatever it was. No good fooling about where Eileen's safety was concerned, though it would go against the grain to bargain with these people.

Five to twelve.

He got up and put on a loose tweed overcoat and a cap. Might as well take the revolver, just in case. He went over to the door and opened it cautiously. He would have to be very quiet. Mrs. Shannon was most likely still awake, and he didn't want to bring her out and have to go into explanations.

He went softly along the passage to the staircase and crept carefully down to the hall. There was an electric torch on the hall table that he had left in readiness, and picking this up he opened the front door. It was bright moonlight outside — the torch would be unnecessary. It had only been a precaution in case it should cloud over. He slipped it into his pocket, shut the door gently behind him, and made his way across the lawn.

He reached the Abbot's Gate — an iron-studded door of aged oak — and pulled back the bolts with difficulty. The door creaked slightly as he opened it and peered out.

'Colonel Shannon?' a low husky voice whispered, and a man stepped forward from the side of the door.

'Yes,' said the colonel curtly, and he took stock of the other. He was muffled to the ears in a heavy overcoat, and a wide-brimmed hat was pulled down over his eyes. Beneath this he wore something that completely covered his face — it looked like a dark handkerchief or scarf.

'You're punctual,' remarked the stranger. 'I have your word that you haven't shown or mentioned my letter to anyone?'

'You have my word,' said Colonel Shannon stiffly.

'Good, then we can get to business. I regret any worry or trouble that the disappearance of your daughter may have caused you, and I'm prepared to guarantee her safe return if you agree to do what I ask.'

'How much do you want?'

'Nothing. The thing I'm going to ask of you has nothing whatever to do with money.'

'Then what the devil do you want?'

'I want you and your wife and your son to take a short holiday,' replied the other smoothly. 'I don't mind in the least where you go, so long as it's some distance from Monk's Ferry. You can remain away for, say, two weeks. At the end of that time you can come back. As soon as you do, your daughter will be returned to you safe and in good health.'

Colonel Shannon stared in astonishment. 'You . . . you want me to take my family away for a fortnight's holiday? What the devil for?'

'That's my business. I shall also require that you arrange for the servants to leave, too, and that you place the keys of the house behind the Abbot's Stone in your garden. It isn't a very big request to make, is it?'

'I don't understand . . . ' began the bewildered colonel.

'There's no reason why you *should*

understand, or try to understand,' he said sharply. 'I've made myself perfectly clear. All you have to do is agree. The alternative to agreeing, of course, is that you will never see your daughter again — alive.'

Colonel Shannon choked back an angry retort. 'How do I know that you'll keep your word?' he demanded.

'You'll have to risk that. I might point out to you that your daughter is of no earthly use to me except as a means of forcing you to do what I ask. I shall be exceedingly glad to be rid of her.'

'When do you want me to start this holiday?' asked the colonel after a slight pause.

'At once. Just as soon as you can make the necessary arrangements.'

Colonel Shannon hesitated. He had been prepared for almost any request but this. 'Very well,' he said grudgingly. 'I agree to your request.'

'Then you'll find your daughter waiting for you in the house when you get back — provided, of course that you don't talk about this to anyone. In that case

. . . well, I've already warned you of the consequences.'

'I'll say nothing,' asserted Colonel Shannon.

'I accept your word,' said the unknown man politely. 'I needn't keep you any longer. Good night.' He walked away quickly, leaving Colonel Shannon, more bewildered than he had ever been in his life, to close and re-bolt the Abbot's Gate and retrace his steps to the house.

17

Peter Walton Makes an Accusation

The next few days went slowly by without anything happening to further Mr. Budd's investigations. Peter Walton's sensational story of the disappearance of Eileen Shannon duly appeared on the front page of the *Post-Courier*, together with a photograph of the missing woman and a detailed description, but the practical result was nil. The editor of that enterprising newspaper received quite a number of letters from misguided people who thought they had seen her, but on investigation these were all found to refer to someone else. Neither did the patient work of the police produce any results whatever. Eileen Shannon had vanished as completely as though she had dissolved into the chemical constituents from which she was made.

Sergeant Leek, assisted by his confrere

from Barnford, continued to keep a zealous watch on Abbot's Rest, without any reward for his labours. Spooky Withers seemed to have settled down for a long stay, and was seen sometimes in company with Major Snodland, sometimes alone, and often with both Snodland and Mrs. Claydon, enjoying the spring air of the countryside; but neither he nor his two companions did anything that was at all suspicious. They were apparently as innocent of wrong-doing as the dog Bisto who accompanied them on their rambles.

Mr. Budd, still holding on to the theory he had outlined to Gordon Ashford with the tenacity and desperation of a drunken man clinging to an even drunker companion, set in motion all the complicated machinery of Scotland Yard to try and trace the man Jackson whom Marie had sent for on his death-bed. He was certain this man held the key to the riddle, even if he was not himself responsible for the killing of little Lew Cator and the murder of Lloyd Gibbs. But it was like looking for a speck of dust in the Sahara Desert. He had no description of Jackson or any other facts to go on at all, except that he had come from Brixton and must have been a very intimate friend of Marie's for the latter to have made him a confidante, which was the basis of the superintendent's idea.

Everitt Marie, when he had found the key, had discovered the hiding-place of the twelve silver statues, but his arrest had prevented him from profiting from his discovery. He had gone to prison to serve his sentence for fraud, hoping that when he came out he would be able to secure this enormous treasure and retrieve his lost fortunes. The secret of the whereabouts of the statues he had kept until he was dying, when he had passed it on to Jackson — or, rather, had passed on the fact that the hiding-place was connected with the Abbot's Key — and this had started the whole train of events which, beginning with the murder of Lew Cator, had led to the murder of Gibbs, the attempted burglary at Abbotsway, and the abduction of Eileen Shannon.

Why Gibbs had been killed, and why Eileen had been taken, were questions he could not answer, but he felt pretty confident that they would answer themselves when the rest became clear. Jackson was the keystone of the edifice, and when he was found the whole building would become firm and solid.

Except for what he had said to Gordon Ashford, the detective had kept his own counsel. He had mentioned nothing of his theory to Peter Walton, in spite of that enterprising young man's repeated efforts to pick his brains and find out what was at the back of his mind. He had no wish for his ideas to leak out and put the unknown Jackson on his guard, which a chance word could quite easily do. It was obvious that without the Abbot's Key, which seemed to have disappeared, Jackson knew no more where the silver saints were hidden than Mr. Budd himself. And it was equally obvious that he would use every endeavour to find the key, which he evidently believed was somewhere at Abbotsway. It was only reasonable to suppose that having made one abortive effort, he would make a further attempt to get it, and Mr. Budd was hoping that this would bring him into the open.

So Mr. Budd waited, filling in his time by acquiring from his new friend Gordon Ashford a comprehensive knowledge of the past history of Monk's Ferry and its inhabitants, and learning much concerning its present. The first news of any importance reached him through Mr. Jephcott while he was at breakfast one morning. The landlord came into the coffee-room and greeted his guest cheerily.

'Good morning, sir,' he said, 'and a very good morning it is to be sure.'

Mr. Budd, slowly consuming his second egg, agreed that it was.

'I s'pose there's no news of Miss Shannon?' inquired Mr. Jephcott rhetorically. 'Terrible thing for the colonel and his lady. I know 'ow I should feel if it were one o' my gals. I expect that's why they're going away.'

'Going away?' said Mr. Budd quickly.

'So the baker tells me. They've cancelled all deliveries of bread and milk for a fortnight. Going away for a change,

194

so they say. I s'pose the house reminds 'em too much of their daughter.'

'When do they go?' asked the detective interestedly.

'This afternoon, I believe. Catching the 4.35 from Barnford.'

Mr. Budd continued to eat his breakfast, his mind very busy indeed. So the Shannons were going away, were they? That would mean that Abbotsway would be empty — or were the servants remaining? He put the question casually to Mr. Jephcott.

'The servants have got a fortnight's holiday, too,' said the landlord. 'Bream and his wife are going to visit their daughter, who's in service with a lady in London. They're shutting the house up.'

Shutting the house up! Mr. Budd pursed his lips. What a piece of luck for — *somebody*. What better opportunity could the person who was after the Abbot's Key have than an empty house?

Mr. Jephcott departed on his lawful business, and Mr. Budd went on with his breakfast, eating mechanically.

An empty house! Could anything better

have happened for the unknown? But what had induced Colonel Shannon and his family to suddenly decide to leave? Their daughter had been spirited away and there was no news of her, and they had decided to go away. Mr. Budd shook his head and absently poured out another cup of tea. It didn't ring true somehow. Torn with anxiety, as both the colonel and his wife undoubtedly were, they would definitely *not* go on a holiday. And yet they were going away that evening, and the servants were going too — leaving an empty house . . .

The detective pushed his cup aside and sought the inspiration of one of his inevitable cigars. And suddenly through the smoke he conjured up a picture of that morning when, in the cold light of dawn, he had watched Colonel Shannon opening a letter brought in by Bream — the unexpected letter which the colonel had stated was an account from the newsagent, but which Mr. Budd had been certain was nothing of the kind. Was that the real reason for Eileen Shannon's abduction? Had she been taken in order

196

to force this result?

'Hm,' Mr. Budd murmured. 'I believe that's what's happened. Clever — very clever indeed.' He got up and strolled thoughtfully to the door. As he reached it, Peter Walton came in.

'Hello,' greeted the reporter. 'You're early this morning. What are you going to do today?'

'Mind my own business,' said Mr. Budd. 'It 'ud be a good idea if you tried doin' the same.'

'All right, I will,' Peter declared, going over to the table and sitting down. 'I was going to tell you something that I thought would interest you, but I shan't now.'

'Withholding information from the police is a serious offence,' said Mr. Budd severely. 'If you know anything that's likely to help in this business, it's your duty to tell me.'

'I don't know that I intend to tell you,' said the reporter coolly. '*You* won't tell *me* anything.'

'Well, make up your mind,' growled Mr. Budd, 'because I can't hang about here all day. I've got a lot to do.'

'Carry on,' said Peter with a wave of his hand. 'I don't suppose you'd be very interested to know who killed Lloyd Gibbs, anyhow.'

'What's that?' demanded Mr. Budd sharply.

'Better sit down. All that weight on your legs can't be good.'

Mr. Budd sat down. 'Now, then, let's have it,' he said. 'Who killed Gibbs?'

'Michael Shannon,' answered the reporter calmly. 'And his sister knew it.'

'How did you get hold of this nonsense?'

'You'll agree that it's not nonsense when you've heard what I have to say.'

'Well, go ahead,' grunted Mr. Budd, 'an' get this fairy tale off your chest.'

'All right. Just wait while I order some breakfast, and I'll tell you all about it.'

18

The Motive?

'When you wouldn't discuss this business with me,' said Peter Walton, talking and eating at the same time, 'I decided that I'd do a bit of nosing about on my own. You were giving your well-known imitation of an oyster and I couldn't get you to open up, so there was nothing else to do.'

'Cut the cackle and get to the horses,' grunted Mr. Budd impatiently.

'Well, as I was saying, I thought I'd do a bit of nosing about on my own. I didn't quite know where to begin, but I concluded that if I talked to enough people, sooner or later I'd hit on something that was worthwhile. And I did. I discovered from one of the lads of the village, a chap called Hamm — and a very appropriate name, too, by the way, in more senses than one — that Michael Shannon was in the habit of sneaking out at night and popping over to Barnford.

'There's a kind of roadhouse just outside the town called The Black Cat. It's rather a dingy place that used to be a private house, but was taken over by a gentleman with a large nose named Jacob Wursman two years ago, who knocked the ground-floor rooms into one, splashed the walls with gaudy paint, and opened the place as a club.

'It's the usual thing — bad food, bad drink, and a small dance band. There are dozens of 'em in London, and this is a sort of poor relation, all very cheap and shoddy, but probably a kind of Aladdin's cave to the youth of Barnford and the district. Anyway, the membership's pretty big, and Wursman must be making quite a nice profit. The joint keeps open until two a.m., and the members eat, drink, and make merry and think themselves fearful dogs.'

'I s'pose we're comin' to somethin' soon?' Mr. Budd sighed.

'You bet we are,' Peter murmured with his mouth full. 'We're coming to it now.' He took a gulp of tea and continued:

'When I heard from Hamm that Michael Shannon was in the habit of going to this place, I pricked up my ears. I was pretty sure the old man knew nothing about it, and although it might have nothing to do with the Gibbs business, I thought it was worth following up.

'I went over to Barnford and got hold of Wursman. He's rather like a clean-shaven gorilla, except for his nose, which is as big as a young elephant's trunk. He was inclined to be a bit terse at first — refused to discuss his members and all that sort of thing; but after I reminded him about a little place he used to run back of Piccadilly Circus, and a certain unpleasantness that he'd been involved in, he was eating out of my hand. It appeared that Michael Shannon was a member of The Black Cat and had been for nearly eighteen months. He used to come to the club about three times a week, and was rather partial to a certain blonde dance hostess. And that wasn't all. He had introduced Lloyd Gibbs to the club and had come with him, three times.'

Peter paused and looked at Mr. Budd

with an expression that plainly said, *What do you think of that?*

'Why didn't this feller come forward and say that Gibbs had been to this place,' Mr. Budd demanded, 'and with young Shannon?'

'Is it likely he would? He wouldn't want the police nosing about round his club and getting the place mixed up with a murder. Naturally he didn't say anything.'

'Go on,' said Mr. Budd. 'But the fact that Michael Shannon took Gibbs to this club is no proof that he murdered him.'

'Wait until you've heard it all,' said Peter dramatically. 'When I found that Michael Shannon and Gibbs had been acquainted, I got a bit excited. And I got even more excited when I learned that there had been a row between them on the night before the murder.'

'What sort of a row?'

'A pretty big one,' said Peter, who knew that his companion, in spite of his placid exterior, was getting interested. 'A row that nearly ended in a fight. In fact, Wursman was so apprehensive about it that they were both asked to leave, and did.'

'What was this row about?'

'The blonde dance hostess. Michael apparently regarded this woman as his special property — not, I understand, without reason — and Gibbs started getting a bit fresh with her. He'd had too much of the stuff they sell as whisky, and anyway, he was always partial to blondes. This woman isn't bad to look at, definitely the type to turn the head of a youngster like Michael, who probably thinks she's the love of his life.

'Anyway, Gibbs and Michael slung blood-curdling threats at each other, and were still slinging 'em when they were practically chucked out. On the following night — the night of the murder — Michael came into The Black Cat just after half-past eleven and demanded to know if Gibbs had been there. When he was told that he hadn't, he sat himself down, ordered a drink and waited, glowering at the entrance and obviously in a very bad temper. The woman, Mavis Gayling, who was the cause of all the trouble, sat out two dances with him and says that he was in a cold fury with Gibbs and swore he was going to 'smash him to pieces'. He left at twelve o'clock, telling Mavis that he was going to find Gibbs and 'have it out'.'

Peter pushed aside his plate and lighted a cigarette. 'And that's not all,' he continued significantly. 'On the night of the murder, Michael Shannon didn't come home until the small hours of the morning. His clothes were dusty and rumpled, and there was a cut on his chin as though he'd been fighting.'

'How do you know that?' asked Mr. Budd quickly.

'From the Shannons' servant. She saw him. Colonel Shannon sent Michael up to shave and wash before he'd let him go in to breakfast. Now shall I tell you what *I* think happened? I think that Michael Shannon, burning with rage at Gibbs, met him near the ruins and, instead of 'smashing him to pieces' as he said he was going to do, stabbed him. And I think that Eileen Shannon, looking out of her window — as we're certain she did in spite of her denial — saw her brother leaving the ruins immediately after the scream and guessed what he'd done.' He stopped, a trifle breathless, and looked triumphantly at Mr. Budd.

That stout and sleepy-eyed man said nothing for a long time. 'There's a lot o' loose ends,' he eventually murmured softly. 'F'instance, how did Michael Shannon get into such a state as you say he was in? There was no struggle an' therefore there was no fight. An' where did he get the knife? An' what was Gibbs doin' near the ruins at that time o' night?'

'Why not let Michael Shannon do the explaining?' said the reporter. 'You've got enough grounds to arrest him on suspicion.'

'Maybe I have,' said Mr. Budd thoughtfully, 'but I'm not goin' to — not yet, anyhow.'

'What more *do* you want?' Peter demanded. 'A written confession, signed, sealed, and witnessed?'

'That 'ud be very handy, Walton,' murmured the superintendent placidly. 'But I don't think the signature'd be Michael Shannon's.'

'I wish,' said Peter suddenly, 'that you'd

open up. What *have* you got in the back of your mind?'

'So many things,' replied Mr. Budd, yawning wearily, 'that it's gettin' a bit congested. I'll open up, as you call it, Walton, when I've got somethin' to open up about. At present it's rather like searchin' fer two or three people in the crowd at a lord mayor's show. I'm not doin' anything that I've got to undo, an' if I detained young Shannon, I'm pretty sure I'd 'ave ter let him go again. But I'd like a word with this feller at The Black Cat, and the gal, too.'

'So you *do* think there's something in it.'

'I think there's a lot in it,' remarked Mr. Budd, getting up ponderously. 'I think there's one most important thing in it that you don't seem to have bothered about.'

'What's that?'

'Why did Michael Shannon take Lloyd Gibbs to this Black Cat place at all? How did they become acquainted? That's what *I* think's important, Walton. An' I think it's so important that I'm goin' to find out before I do anythin' else.'

19

The Dance Hostess

The Black Cat was very much as Peter Walton had described it. At one time it had been a house of some pretentions, built in the Elizabethan period, and with a fair acreage of ground. The greater part of this, however, had been bought by a speculative builder who had erected bungalows of the cheaper type, and all that now belonged to the house was a small front garden and drive and a tiny patch of ground at the rear. The inside was terrible. The enterprising Mr. Jacob Wursman had completely modernized it, using a glaring colour scheme in the process that seemed to consist of every shade of red, orange and green.

Mr. Budd stood and gaped at all this magnificence, a little dazed at so much colour in bulk, and thought of his beloved roses in the small garden at Streatham.

He was waiting to see Mr. Wursman, his card having been taken up to that gentleman's office by the porter. After a short interval the porter returned, followed by a short fat man with a bald head and a prodigious nose. He came over to Mr. Budd, nervously twisting the card between stubby fingers.

'You are Superintendent Budd?' he asked, and when the big man nodded: 'I hope there isn't any trouble . . . '

'I hope so, too,' said Mr. Budd. 'If you're Mr. Wursman, I'd just like to ask you a few questions concernin' Mr. Lloyd Gibbs, who was murdered the other night at Monk's Ferry.'

'I know nothing about him,' said Mr. Wursman hastily. 'He was brought to the club by a member once or twice, that's all. I know absolutely nothing about him.'

'There's no need for you to go gettin' upset,' said Mr. Budd reassuringly. 'I'm not suggestin' that you know anythin' about him. All I'm askin' you to do is to give a straight answer to some straight questions, that's all.'

'I'll do anything I can, of course,' said

Mr. Wursman ingratiatingly.

'Good. Now, will you tell me the name of the member who brought Mr. Gibbs here?'

'Mr. Michael Shannon,' said the proprietor instantly.

'An' how many times did he bring Mr. Gibbs?'

'Three times altogether.'

'Mr. Shannon didn't meet Mr. Gibbs here?' said the detective, sleepily eyeing a hideous-looking nymph with spindly legs and a flat chest dancing on the wall in front of him. 'You're sure Mr. Shannon brought 'im?'

'Quite sure,' declared Mr. Wursman. 'Mr. Gibbs was not a member. Mr. Shannon signed him in each time.'

'I see. Now, on the last occasion that they was here, there was a bit of a bother, wasn't there?'

'Just a little trouble — nothing serious. The two gentlemen had taken a little too much to drink and had an argument.'

'It was over a gal, wasn't it? A gal called Mavis Gayling, who's employed here as a dancin' partner.'

'Who *was* employed here,' corrected Mr. Wursman. 'Miss Gayling is no longer employed here. She was sacked. I paid her a week's money in lieu of notice and told her to clear out.'

'You did?' murmured Mr. Budd. 'Why did you sack 'er?'

Mr. Wursman shrugged. 'I can't have people making trouble. I like to keep my establishment respectable.'

'The gal wasn't to blame, was she?'

'Well, no,' admitted the proprietor. 'But she was the cause. Mr. Shannon took rather a violent fancy to her and resented other people's attentions to her. That was no good to me. She was engaged to make herself pleasant to everybody, you understand? It wasn't good business.'

'Where's Miss Gayling now?'

'She had rooms in Barnford. Whether she's still there or not, I couldn't say.'

'She doesn't live in Barnford?'

Mr. Wursman shook his head. 'No, no, she's a London woman. She came to live in Barnford when I engaged her.' He gave Mr. Budd the address of her lodgings, and the detective noted it down.

'Now,' said Mr. Budd, putting away his pocketbook, 'there's just one other question, Mr. Wursman. Have you any idea how Mr. Shannon an' Mr. Gibbs became acquainted?'

The proprietor had no idea. He knew nothing whatever about either of them, and he quite obviously did not *want* to know anything. His one desire was not to be mixed up in anything that would be 'bad for business'.

Mr. Budd, having drawn a blank at The Black Cat — which was no more than he had expected — took his departure, to the very evident relief of its anxious proprietor, and drove to the address of Miss Mavis Gayling. It was in a respectable street consisting of two rows of houses, all exactly alike, and only distinguishable one from the other by the colour of the curtains and the numbers on the front doors. Miss Gayling's address was number ten, and Mr. Budd knocked on the door, fervently hoping that she was still living there.

She was not only still there, but what was even luckier, she was in. A thin, worried-looking woman with soap-sudded arms opened the door, ushered him into the hall, shouted up the stairs: 'Gen'leman for you, Miss Gayling,' and disappeared with remarkable speed to some remote region at the back.

'Who is it, Mrs. Geddy?' called a woman's voice. Receiving no reply, the owner of the voice came to the top of the staircase and repeated the question.

'You wouldn't know me, miss,' said Mr. Budd in his most avuncular manner, 'but I should like to see you for a moment or two.'

Mavis Gayling looked down at him suspiciously. She was a tall woman with a nice figure and a mass of very light fair hair that she wore loose. 'What do you want to see me about?' she demanded carefully, in a voice that for all its affectedness failed to conceal its Cockney origin.

'Well, now, miss,' answered Mr. Budd, 'it's rather a private matter. If there was somewhere that was a bit less public where we could talk . . . ?'

'You'd better come up for a minute,' she said.

'Thank you, miss.' Mr. Budd mounted the staircase ponderously, hat in hand. She led him into a room on the right of the square landing and closed the door. It was poorly furnished but very clean. A pair of thin silk stockings hung over a chair in front of a gas fire and steamed, showing that they had not long been washed.

'Now,' said Mavis, standing near the door and looking at him steadily, 'what is it?'

Mr. Budd made a quick decision regarding his line of approach. Without beating about the bush, he introduced himself and explained the reason for his visit.

The wary look in her eyes faded. She went over to the mantelpiece, took a cigarette from a half-filled packet, and lit it with a small lighter. 'Why don't you ask Mr. Shannon?' she said, trickling smoke through her nostrils. 'Why come to me?'

'Because,' replied Mr. Budd candidly, 'I believe I shall get more out of you. Don't misunderstand me,' he added quickly, as her expression hardened, 'I don't want you to think that this'll be doin' Mr. Shannon any harm. I don't think that he had anythin' to do with the murder, an' I'm not interested in his relations with the dead man. What I'm interested in is the dead man's relations with him, if you can see what I mean?'

'Yes, I think I do. You want to know why this man Gibbs should have bothered with Mickey at all, isn't that it?'

'That's as near it as makes no matter, miss.'

'Well, I can't tell you,' she said, wrinkling her brows. 'He met Mickey in the village and got into conversation with him — this is what Mickey told me. He seemed to know who he was and where he lived, and went out of his way to be friendly. He asked him a lot of questions about Monk's Ferry and the people who lived there, and about the old ruins. Mickey hadn't many friends — not interesting friends, he wasn't allowed to — and Gibbs, who'd seen a good bit of the world and could tell a good story of his experiences, amused him. I didn't like him,' she added suddenly. 'He was too fond of pawing you about.'

'Who suggested bringin' him to The Black Cat?'

'Mr. Gibbs suggested it when Mickey told him about it,' Mavis answered promptly, 'and I wish to heaven he hadn't brought him. It only led to trouble. You know about that, of course?'

'Yes, I know about that. It was over you, wasn't it?'

'Mickey is . . . well, rather keen on me,' she said, resting her arm on the mantelshelf and staring down at the gas fire. 'Seriously keen, I mean; not just out for a good time like most of the others — you know what I mean? Gibbs had a drink or two and started to get a bit fresh. I could have handled him all right — I'm used to handling that sort.' A shade of bitterness came into her voice. 'But Mickey got all hot and bothered and went off the deep end. There was nearly a fight, and old Wursman made them both leave.' She inhaled the smoke of her cigarette deeply and flung the remainder of it in the fender. 'That's about all I can tell you.' She looked up at him candidly.

'I rather thought it was somethin' like that, miss,' Mr. Budd murmured. 'That Gibbs struck up an acquaintance with Mr. Shannon an' not the other way round. What was all these questions he asked about Monk's Ferry?'

'Mickey never told me. He only said that he was always asking questions about the place and its history.'

'Did he ever mention the Twelve Apostles?'

Her thin eyebrows shot up in surprise. 'I shouldn't think so,' she said in astonishment. 'That's the last thing that'd interest a man like Gibbs.'

The superintendent saw that she had never heard of the legend attached to Monk's Ferry and Felsbank Abbey, and he made no attempt to explain.

'Has anything been heard of Mickey's sister?' she asked abruptly.

'No, nothin', miss. It's a very queer business.'

'It's horrible. Horrible! Mickey wrote and told me. They were all very upset.'

'The Shannons are goin' away,' said Mr. Budd thoughtfully. 'For a holiday.'

Mavis was startled. He saw her face suddenly whiten until the rouge on her cheeks stood out in ragged red patches. 'Going away?' she cried. 'When — for how long?'

'They're leavin' this afternoon. I don't know for how long.'

'I suppose Colonel Shannon arranged it,' she said vindictively. 'I'm sure nobody else would have thought of going away at a time like this. Something ought to be done to that man. He's impossible.'

'You're very fond of Mr. Michael Shannon, ain't you, miss?' interrupted Mr. Budd gently.

'Of Mickey? Why, I . . . ' She stopped suddenly, and the colour flooded back to her face in a great wave. 'Why, yes I am.' She ended lamely, 'Very fond of him.'

Mr. Budd took his leave, having ascertained that Mavis Gayling would not be leaving Barnford for another week. He had not learned much, but what he had seemed to confirm his preconceived opinion. As his ancient car bumped him uncomfortably back to Monk's Ferry, he wondered what it was that Mavis Gayling had been going to say when she had suddenly pulled herself up and said something entirely different.

20

The Smell of Incense

Mr. Budd called at Long Meadow Farm on his way back to The Monk's Head and found Gordon Ashford at home. He was introduced to Mrs. Ashford, a charming old lady with silver hair and one of those gentle faces on which age seems to linger lovingly, and was given tea in a big old-world restful room full of flowers and comfort. Afterwards, Gordon took him along to a small room in which he worked. It contained two easy chairs, a large desk, a big filing cabinet, and very little else. Here, ensconced in one of the chairs, which he filled completely, Mr. Budd smoked a cigar and gave an abridged account of all that had happened since he had last seen his newfound friend. Gordon listened with interest, though it was obvious that he was bitterly disappointed that the superintendent had no news of Eileen to offer.

'I know Michael used to slip out at night and go over to this place at Barnford,' he said. 'So did Eileen. She was rather worried about it, because if the old man found out, there would have been one hell of a row. He would never have stood for it for a moment.'

Mr. Budd agreed with him. Colonel Shannon would never have understood that the rigid strictness with which he had brought up his children had forced them to seek a clandestine outlet to counteract the drabness of their lives. 'I s'pose you know,' he said, glancing at the clock on the desk, 'that the Shannons have gone away?'

Gordon Ashford's reaction was even more marked than Mavis Gayling's had been.

'Gone away? What on earth do you mean?'

Mr. Budd explained.

'I knew nothing about it,' declared Gordon. 'I haven't been away from the farm all day, and I've heard nothing. Good God, Shannon must be mad.'

'I don't think he's mad at all,' said Mr.

Budd, and he proceeded to tell Gordon of his opinion concerning the letter which the colonel had received.

'So that's it,' Ashford said. 'You believe these people have used Eileen as a means for getting the house empty so that they can search for the Abbot's Key?'

'I do, an' that's what I'm here for, Mr. Ashford. I want your help.'

'You've got it. What can I do?'

'You can meet me tonight at the ruins of the old abbey. About ten o'clock 'ull do.'

'What for?'

'Abbotsway 'ull be empty, but I'd like ter make sure that it won't be unguarded. I'm very curious to see what happens when that place is empty, Mr. Ashford.'

A sparkle of excitement came into Gordon's eyes. 'You mean that the seeker for the Abbot's Key might put in a little research work.'

Mr. Budd nodded. 'I think he might,' he murmured, 'an' I'd like to be there if he does — just ter give him a welcome.'

'But why the ruins? Aren't they rather far away?'

'It's a good meetin' place, nice an'

handy. I'm not suggestin' we stop there. I think *inside* the house is the place to receive the visitor — if he comes, an' I don't think that 'ull be before ten o'clock.'

'I'll be there,' said Gordon.

'Maybe the ghost 'ull be there, too,' said Mr. Budd, yawning. 'Well, seein' as how I look like bein' up fer the greater part of the night, I think I'll go an' have a bit of sleep.'

★ ★ ★

An uncertain moon shone hazily at irregular intervals through a scrabble of cloud, and a north wind blew coldly across the open country. There was rain in the air. Abbotsway, alternately flooded with pale light and plunged into darkness, stood silent and deserted among the whispering trees, appearing and disappearing like the dissolving shots in a film on a cinema screen.

The Shannons had gone, and, later in the evening, had been followed by Bream and his wife and the servant Annie, all rather bewildered by this sudden exodus on the part of the family. The old house, empty, and cold, and shuttered for the first time in four years, sank gently into a drowsy peacefulness, as dead and lifeless as the ruins of the ancient abbey it faced. The moon, weaving a silver weft among the woof of cloud, touched the spring flowers in the garden to startled life and whitened the Abbot's Stone to virgin purity. It lit up the road intermittently, as Mr. Budd, enveloped in a heavy overcoat, set forth from The Monk's Head to keep his appointment with Gordon Ashford.

There had been no sign of Peter Walton, for which he was very thankful. He had no desire for the reporter's company on the night's excursion, and if Peter had got wind of it there would have been no keeping him away. Mr. Jephcott had been very curious to know how things were going, but the big man skilfully parried all his questions.

At half-past nine he had left the inn and started on his walk to the ruins, and in the pocket of his overcoat he carried a compact automatic pistol, fully loaded. It was unusual for him to carry a weapon of any sort — police regulations frowned on such a practice — but the seeker for the Abbot's Key was a dangerous man and Mr. Budd preferred to be prepared for all eventualities.

He reached the gloomy ruins of Felsbank Abbey at exactly ten, a little breathless from his unaccustomed exercise, to find Gordon Ashford already waiting. 'I don't s'pose anything 'ull happen for some time,' whispered the superintendent. 'He's almost sure to leave it until pretty late, if he comes at all. He may think it safer to wait for a night or two.'

'What do we do, then?' inquired Gordon.

'Possess ourselves of patience an' keep a sharp look out,' grunted Mr. Budd. 'One thing's certain — he'll come sooner or later.'

The moon at that moment was making one of its transient appearances, and he looked round at the heaps of tumbled stones, the half-destroyed square tower, and the great arch thrusting up forlornly into the night sky. 'Queer how things change,' he murmured philosophically. 'You can almost imagine this place as it was — a great abbey, solid an' lookin' as though it 'ud last for ever, as I expect those monks thought it would when they built it. An' now it's almost gone.'

Gordon was surprised. The stolid, lethargic, rather plebeian-looking man before him did not look imaginative. And yet he supposed he must possess a certain amount of imagination to be successful in his profession.

'It must have been quite an impressive place,' went on Mr. Budd. ''Specially the great hall with them life-sized silver statues standin' in twelve niches an' the monks chantin' their vespers, or whatever it was they chanted. It sort o' makes this murder worse, don't it? Like sacrilege.'

The moonlight faded slowly, and the ruins of the abbey dissolved into the gloom.

'Well,' said Mr. Budd, suddenly becoming practical, 'I s'pose we'd better be gettin' on with the job. Come on.'

'Listen.' Gordon laid a hand on his arm. '*Listen.*'

'What is it? I can't hear anythin'.'

'I thought I heard a faint sound,' said Gordon under his breath. 'Like voices. Can't you hear it now? It's like men chanting.'

It came: attenuated ghostly music, scarcely audible above the sighing of the wind, as though from far away — a distant choir. Mr. Budd heard it and his flesh crept. 'Where's it comin' from?' he asked softly.

Gordon shook his head. 'I don't know,' he breathed. 'It seems everywhere — above, below, and all around us.' He looked uneasily about, but there was nothing visible, only that faint chanting that could scarcely be heard. And now there was something else. The wind carried it to their nostrils and wafted it away. It was like the opening of an old box in which the trace of an ancient perfume still lingers — the spicy, unmistakable smell of incense.

'Good God!' Gordon Ashford's white face glimmered in the dark close to Mr. Budd's. 'What . . . *what is it?*'

They stood silent in the gloom, a little awed, listening while the muted, muffled cadence of the chanting voices floated round them, filling the darkness with a faint and distant echo of a sound that must, centuries before, have been common enough in that place. And the air was full of the smell of incense . . .

21

A Night at Abbotsway

Mr. Budd was the first to pull himself out of the spell that had gripped them both. 'We're behavin' like a couple o' nervous old ladies,' he said disgustedly. 'There must be some natural explanation for these things.'

'What explanation can there be?' said Gordon. 'We didn't imagine the chanting or the incense. You heard it and smelt it as well as I did. You can hear it and smell it now.'

'I know, an' we've got ter find out what the cause is. I wish this infernal moon 'ud come out.'

The 'infernal moon' most graciously obliged at that moment and sailed free of a bank of cloud. It was almost as if the detective had uttered a magic formula. He took advantage of the light to make, with the help of Gordon, a hasty search of the ruins. Before they could entirely complete it the moon had gone again, but they had done enough to assure themselves that nobody was there playing any kind of trick. Except for themselves, the ruins were deserted.

'Well, that's that,' grunted Mr. Budd, breathing heavily from his exertions. 'I can't hear anythin' now, can you?'

Gordon listened intently for a second and then shook his head. 'No, I can't hear anything, but I can still smell the incense.'

A large drop of rain fell on Mr. Budd's hand and startled him. It was followed by another and another until it was pattering around them heavily. 'That settles it,' said Mr. Budd decisively. 'I'm not goin' to stay here an' get wet through fer all the chantin' and incense in the world. Come on, Ashford, we'll get over to the house as quickly as we can.'

He set off at a lumbering trot, and Gordon, by no means loath to leave the ruins, strode along at his side. It was raining in torrents by the time they had crossed the bed of the River Fell, and they were both glad to reach the house.

'This way,' panted Mr. Budd as Gordon was making for the front entrance. 'We haven't got a key, you know. We'll have to do a bit of burglin' to get in.'

He led the way round to the back, found a window that was un-shuttered, and after some difficulty succeeded in forcing it open. 'You go first,' he said to Gordon, 'an' then you can help me through.'

Ashford swung himself quickly across the sill and turned to assist Mr. Budd. He found that this was by no means an easy task. Eventually, however, the big man was got through the window and arrived inside, gasping and floundering like a newly landed fish.

They were in a small room near the kitchen that had been used as a storage place for odds and ends. Outside, when they opened the door, was a passage which led through to the hall. Mr. Budd produced a torch, over the end of which he had secured two thicknesses of tissue-paper so that the light was very dim, and they crept along to the foot of the staircase.

It was pitch dark and the house was very still. A faint trace of cigar smoke lingered in the air, and the big clock against one wall ticked steadily. Mr. Budd sent the light of the torch jumping from side to side.

'There's no sayin' how long we may have to wait,' he whispered, 'so we may as well be comfortable. There's a couple o' chairs over there.' He went over and sat down, and Gordon followed him.

'I think this is the best place for us,' continued the superintendent. 'It's central, an' we'll hear any sound when this feller comes.'

'I wonder if he'll come tonight,' said Gordon.

Mr. Budd shrugged. 'Maybe, an' maybe not. Since he's taken all this trouble to get the house empty, he won't want to waste any time.'

'Do you think the Abbot's Key is here?'

'*He* thinks it is, an' that's the main thing. We might have a look for it ourselves in the daylight. I'd rather like to get hold of that thing.'

'If it *is* here. I can't understand why Colonel Shannon didn't know anything about it.'

'Well, I don't suppose Marie would have left it lyin' about, an' — '

'Shhh,' whispered Gordon, nudging him sharply. 'What was that?'

They listened. The clock ticked regularly, and outside the rain hissed and pattered. 'I can't hear anythin',' said Mr. Budd, putting his lips close to Gordon's ear.

'I can't now,' answered Gordon, 'but I'm sure I *did* hear something — like a stealthy step on wet gravel.'

They listened again, but there were no sounds other than the rain, the dripping water, and the monotonous tick-tock of the big clock. 'You must've made a mistake,' said Mr. Budd after nearly three long minutes had dragged by.

'I suppose I must,' muttered Gordon. 'But I could have sworn I heard someone outside.'

'It's queer how you can be deceived about things like that, particularly when you're expectin' — ' He broke off and his large body stiffened. This time they both heard something, and there was no mistaking what it was: the soft crunch of feet on wet gravel outside.

Mr. Budd was up with surprising speed and quietness for a man of his bulk, and, gripping Gordon by his coat sleeve, dragged him over to the big staircase and forced him down in the shelter of its massive banisters.

The sound of the footsteps outside changed as they left the path and came onto the stone-flagged porch. Here they stopped, there was a slight scraping noise, and then a rattle of metal. Somebody was fitting a key into the lock of the front door. It turned softly, there was the faintest of faint creaks, and the big door began to swing open slowly. A narrow length of grey light split the intense darkness and gradually widened.

The sound of the falling rain increased in intensity; a blot of shapeless black shadow, as though the darkness of the old house was seeping out and merging with the greyness outside, spread as the door moved wider and wider. There was a pause, and then the dark shadow seemed to surge forward and grow larger.

And then Gordon Ashford's foot

slipped on the polished floor and flew from under him. Over-balancing, he cannoned against Mr. Budd, who only saved himself from falling by flinging out a hand and gripping one of the banisters. He recovered himself and staggered to his feet, but the shadow, looming in the open doorway, heard the noise and took alarm. With a muffled exclamation, it sprang backward and out into the wet night.

As Mr. Budd came to his feet, the vague shape turned and fled across the lawn. For a second a bleared, watery moonlight flooded the garden with a dim radiance, and in the pale, shifting light the detective caught a glimpse of something in a long grey habit and cowl.

'Take this an' go after him,' he grunted urgently and breathlessly, and thrust his automatic into Gordon's hand. 'You can run faster'n I can.'

Gordon grabbed the gun and started in pursuit, but the transient moonlight had gone and he could see nothing through the mist of rain. He reached the gate and came out onto the road, pausing there to listen. But there was no sound. The man of the night had vanished. Wet, and fuming with annoyance at his own clumsiness, he came back to the house and rejoined Mr. Budd.

'No luck,' he said. 'I lost him in the dark. I say, I'm terribly sorry, but I couldn't help it. My foot slipped.'

'It's a pity, but it can't be helped,' said Mr. Budd philosophically. 'I don't s'pose we'll get such another chance, though. He'll be on his guard now.' Did you see how he was dressed — like a monk?'

Gordon nodded.

'Pretty good idea. If any stray person from the village happened ter see him, they wouldn't inquire too closely, an' it makes a good disguise as well. Must've been the same feller who broke in an' scared Miss Shannon.' He closed the front door and switched on the hall light. 'He knows we're here now, so it doesn't matter, an' we might as well see what we're doin'.'

'What are we doing?'

'Lookin' for the Abbot's Key. We may as well try an' get somethin' for all our trouble.'

They began with the ground floor and gradually worked their way through the whole house, but although they found a number of old keys, the Abbot's Key was not among them. Gordon was positive about this, and, since he had actually seen it, he knew what he was talking about.

It was in the early hours of the morning when they finished their search and came back to the hall, weary and dispirited. It was still dark outside, and the rain was falling steadily.

'That feller had a key to the house, did you notice that?' said Mr. Budd, suddenly breaking a long silence. 'There's not much doubt that I'm right about the reason Colonel Shannon took his family away.'

'What will the man in the monk's robe do now?' asked Gordon.

'I don't know. He must be feelin' pretty wild. Havin' gone to all the trouble he did to get the place to himself, an' then to find us waitin' fer him, must've upset him no end. If he comes again, he'll be takin' a big risk, but he must have the key.'

'If *we* can't find the thing, I don't see

how he would stand much chance.'

'Unless he knows where to look,' said Mr. Budd, rubbing his nose. 'Maybe he does.'

'You think Marie hid the key and told this man where?'

'Somethin' of the sort.' The detective gave a prodigious yawn. 'There's nuthin' more we can do here,' he said, looking wearily round. 'We may as well go an' get some sleep.'

He switched out the light and they left by the front door, shutting it carefully behind them. The wind was blowing coldly, and Gordon shivered as they made their way down the sodden path to the gate. The rain had soaked through his coat and he felt damp, clammy, and uncomfortable. The night had not been successful, and it was his fault, a fact that did not add to his cheerfulness.

Outside on the road, Mr. Budd stopped. 'We'll just go over to the ruins for a moment,' he said. 'I'd like to hear if that queer chantin's still goin' on.'

They crossed the dip of the old river and picked their way among the heaps of wet stones. Under the broken arch they stopped and listened. There was no sound now except the rain and the wind, and no other smell except the scent of the wet earth. Mr. Budd took out his torch, pulled the paper off the end, and swept the light from side to side. It danced over the weed-grown pavement and flickered in and out of the piles of grey-black stones.

'What's *that*?' Gordon's voice was suddenly shrill. 'Over there.' He pointed to the ruined cloisters. 'Your light touched something.'

The ray went flashing back, wavered, and came to rest. 'God Almighty!' exclaimed the startled Mr. Budd, and he lumbered hurriedly over.

There *was* something in the shadow of the cloisters — something that lay inert in a muddy puddle that was tinged with red, a pale face upturned to the soaking sky . . .

Rita Claydon — and she was dead!

22

An Interview with Major Snodland

In the cold, wet dawn, with an icy wind blowing fitfully across the open country and driving the rain into their faces, the two men stood in the gaunt ruins of Felsbank Abbey round the dead body of Mrs. Rita Claydon. It was just light — a grey, unpleasant light that added pallor to already pale cheeks and played tricks with the eyesight. Mr. Budd, weary and wet, with his hat a dripping ruin, had been a very busy man since he and Gordon Ashford had made their ghastly discovery.

Leaving his companion to guard the body, the detective had hurried back to Abbotsway, and, gaining admittance by the window through which they had entered before, had sat himself at the telephone and used that instrument to some purpose. The result had been to rouse Superintendent Boyder from his dreams, drag Doctor Lidstone from a warm and comfortable bed, and bring the resentful and reluctant Fowler post-haste on a bicycle.

Before any of them could arrive, Mr. Budd went back to the ruins and made a hasty but thorough examination of the dead woman and the place where she had met her death. Like Lloyd Gibbs, she had been stabbed — an upward thrust in her left side which, judging from the amount of blood, must have pierced one or more of the great vessels of the heart. There was nothing to show who had delivered the thrust, or why she had come to such a lonely place in the early hours of the morning. She was dressed in a plain tweed costume, over which she wore a transparent cape with an attached hood. She carried no handbag, and there was nothing in her pockets.

'She hasn't been dead very long,' said Doctor Lidstone, who had just finished his examination. 'Approximately four hours. It might be less and it might be more, and she died from the effect of a wound administered by a thin-bladed knife that entered her heart. She must have been dead before the weapon could be withdrawn. That's all I can tell you until after the post-mortem.' He glanced down ruefully at his muddy raincoat and grunted. 'If you don't want me anymore, I'll go home and get clean and dry.' He went away in his little car.

Boyder looked at Mr. Budd. 'Well, this is a nice business,' he said gloomily. 'I don't know what the chief constable'll say about it, but it won't be very pleasant.'

'Nuthin' that feller could say 'ud be pleasant,' snarled Mr. Budd, who was beginning to get irritable. 'Never mind him. S'pose we get the body away, an' get ourselves out o' this infernal rain?'

Superintendent Boyder had come prepared with an ambulance, and Fowler, and the constable Boyder had brought with him, lifted the poor bedraggled body of Rita Claydon and carried it over to the waiting vehicle. When the ambulance had driven off in the direction of Barnford, Mr. Budd turned to Fowler. 'You seen anythin' o' Sergeant Leek?' he asked.

'No, sir. He hadn't come in when I left.

I looked in his room, but it was empty.'

'What time does he usually get in?'

'When he's out at night, about five. That's why I looked to see if he was in, sir. He oughter have been.'

'Let's go to Abbot's Rest,' said the detective, addressing Boyder. 'We can use your car. Maybe we'll find Leek there.'

Ever since they had found the body of Rita Claydon, Mr. Budd had been puzzling his brain to know what could have happened either to Leek or the man who was sharing his watch on the inhabitants of Abbot's Rest. Boyder realized what was in his mind as they went over to his car.

'You're wondering how the woman managed to get here without being followed,' he said. It was more a statement than a question.

'I am,' agreed Mr. Budd, frowning. 'I'm wonderin' very much how that could've happened. An' somebody's goin' to be severely ticked off when I find out!'

They clambered into the local superintendent's car and drove away in steamy discomfort. It did not take very long to reach Major Snodland's cottage, and Boyder, at Mr. Budd's direction, stopped the car by a clump of trees a few yards away.

'One or other of 'em ought to be here somewhere,' the detective said, and he hoisted himself out. But there was no sign of anybody. He walked a little further along the road, peering into the trees that formed a small copse opposite the cottage. No one. And then as he turned to go back, a man appeared suddenly from nowhere.

'You're Superintendent Budd, ain't you, sir?' he said, and when Mr. Budd nodded: 'I'm Dawson, Sergeant Leek's relief.'

'Where *is* Sergeant Leek?' demanded the detective impatiently.

'That's what I'd like to know, sir. 'E should've been 'ere when I came to relieve 'im, but 'e wasn't.'

'What time was that?'

'Five o'clock, sir. And 'e wasn't 'ere.'

'Has anyone come out of or gone into Abbot's Rest since you've been here?' Mr. Budd inquired.

'No, sir.'

'Where do you keep watch from?'

'Over there, sir.' Dawson pointed to a clump of trees at the junction of Meadow Lane and the Abbotsway road. 'You can see both the back and front of the cottage from there.'

Mr. Budd grunted, a little perplexed and more than a little annoyed. What had happened to the melancholy Leek? Had he seen Rita Claydon leave the cottage and followed her? If that was the case, where the devil was he?

A sudden suspicion occurred to him. Supposing that Leek *had* followed her to the ruins, and run afoul of the murderer. Supposing he had suffered the same fate as Gibbs and Rita Claydon . . . But in that event, surely they would have found his body.

An alternative suggested itself. Supposing Leek had seen the murder and was on the track of the murderer. This seemed the more likely. Leek had followed the woman, witnessed the crime, and was trailing the murderer. Mr. Budd nodded to himself. That was what must have happened. In which case, he ought to be hearing from the lean sergeant very soon.

'All right, Dawson,' he said. 'Go back to your post. I'm goin' to have a few words with this Major Snodland.'

''As anything 'appened, sir?'

'Murder,' said Mr. Budd briefly, and left him gaping in open-mouthed surprise. He went back to the car, and in a few words acquainted Boyder with what he thought had happened.

'That's about it,' agreed the local man. 'Yes, I should say you're right. It'll be a good thing if you are, because we ought to have this murderer under lock an' key in a few hours.'

'Maybe we will,' said Mr. Budd. 'In the meanwhile, I think we'll pay a visit to this feller Snodland.'

Boyder agreed, and leaving Gordon in the car, got out and accompanied the detective to the cottage. They walked up the strip of path and knocked at the front door. A tremendous outcry of muffled barking came from within. The dog, Bisto, was evidently justifying his existence. Mr. Budd waited a moment or two and then knocked again, louder and more peremptorily.

The barking increased, a voice said 'Be *quiet*, damn you,' and then the door was opened and the red face of Major Snodland peered out. 'Who is it — what the devil do you want?' he demanded huskily and irritably.

Mr. Budd introduced Boyder and himself in his most official tone. 'We'd like a word with you, sir. It concerns a lady who's been stayin' with you, a Mrs. Rita Claydon.'

'What business is it of yours who's staying with me?' said Snodland, still peering round the side of the door.

'I think you'll find it's very much our business, sir,' put in Boyder sternly. 'The lady's body was found early this morning in the ruins of Felsbank Abbey.'

Major Snodland gave a startled gasp and the red faded from his rather bloated face, leaving behind a queer, blotchy yellow. He opened the door wider, licked his lips, and said in a voice huskier than ever: 'You'd better come in.'

He led the way into a comfortable

room on the left of the tiny hall, shut the door and stood by it, staring almost stupidly at them. Mr. Budd saw that he was fully dressed, but that his ginger hair was dishevelled and he was unshaven. Major Snodland had quite evidently not been to bed that night.

'What's this you say?' he muttered at length. 'Rita . . . Mrs. Claydon . . . ' He stopped, mumbling incoherently, his boiled-sweet eyes protruding more than usual. 'How — how did it happen?'

'Mrs. Claydon was murdered,' said Mr. Budd bluntly, 'an' we've reason to believe that she was murdered by the same person or persons who killed Lloyd Gibbs.'

Snodland raised a swollen, shaking hand and fingered his strip of moustache. 'Murdered,' he said in a hoarse whisper.

'I'm afraid so, sir. An' since the lady was a friend o' yours, it'll be necessary later for you to make a formal identification of her body. In the meanwhile, we should be glad if you'd answer a few questions.'

Snodland nodded dully. He looked

dazed and not a little scared.

'How long have you known Mrs. Claydon?' asked the detective.

'Not very long. Nine or ten months.'

'I see. Hm. An' how long has she been stayin' here with you?'

'For ten or twelve days. I can't remember exactly. Not more.'

'Was her visit to you just a friendly one, or did you have any business relations with her?'

'Her visit was just a friendly one,' said Major Snodland reluctantly.

'Are you acquainted with any of Mrs. Claydon's relations — her husband, f'instance?'

'No, I believe she was divorced . . . I don't know . . . I really know very little about her.'

'But you were sufficiently friendly with her for her to be stayin' here as your guest?'

'Yes.' Snodland seemed to find difficulty in speaking and cleared his throat. 'Do you . . . do you mind if I have a drink? This . . . this has been rather a shock.'

Mr Budd nodded, and the man went

unsteadily over to the sideboard and poured himself out a stiff whisky, which he swallowed neat at a gulp. 'That's better,' he muttered, setting down the empty glass. 'By Jove, I needed that.' The colour came slowly back to his round, fattish face, and his dull eyes brightened a little. 'Would you like a drink?'

'No, thank you, sir,' said Mr. Budd, and Boyder shook his head. 'Can you suggest any reason why anyone should want to kill Mrs. Claydon?'

'No.' Snodland leaned back, both his elbows resting on the sideboard.

'Did she know Lloyd Gibbs?'

'No, I don't think so. Not that I'm aware.'

'But she was acquainted with Marie, wasn't she?'

'Marie?' A slight — very slight — change came over Snodland's face. His eyes became wary.

'Everitt Marie,' explained Mr. Budd carefully. 'The man who used to live at Abbotsway, an' was arrested for fraud.'

'I don't know if she knew him. I've never heard her mention him,' said Major

Snodland slowly.

'Did you know him?'

He shook his head. 'I've heard of him, but I never met him. I've only lived here for two years.' The whisky had taken effect. He was less nervous, but the wary look still lingered in his eyes.

'Why did Mrs. Claydon go out last night?' continued Mr. Budd, to whom by tacit consent Boyder seemed to have left the questioning.

'We had been playing cards until very late.' Snodland was rapidly becoming more and more sure of himself and easy in his manner. 'She had a headache and thought the air would do her good. She said she was going for a walk.'

'In the rain?' Mr. Budd raised his eyebrows.

'Yes. I tried to dissuade her, but you know what women are like.' He shrugged.

'It's a pretty long walk from here to the ruins, isn't it? An' rather a queer place for a woman to choose in the middle of the night.'

'I suppose it is,' answered Snodland noncommittally.

'What time was it when she left?'

Long pause. 'I'm not quite sure,' Snodland answered at last. 'Round about half-past two, I think.'

'What did you do after she'd gone? Did you go to bed?'

'No, I sat up. I had a drink and smoked and waited for her to come in. I must have fallen asleep, because the next thing I remember was hearing you knock.'

Mr. Budd looked at Boyder and stroked his fleshy chin. The story was plausible, but he didn't believe a word of it. It was unlikely that Rita Claydon would have chosen to go for a walk on such a night — and more than unlikely that, even if she had, she would have gone to such an ill-omened place as the ruins of Felsbank Abbey. Major Snodland was lying, but there was no proof of it, and so for the present there was nothing to do but accept his statement.

'You have a man called Withers stayin' with you, haven't you?' said Mr. Budd.

'Yes.' Snodland inclined his ginger head.

'Is he a friend o' yours?'

'No. He came here on a matter of business.'

'Business?' The detective looked at him questioningly. 'What kind o' business?'

'Well, I really don't see — ' began Snodland, but Mr. Budd interrupted him.

'We're investigatin' a murder,' he said sternly. 'An' this man Withers has a criminal record. You may not be aware o' that, but I must ask you to tell me what sort o' business brought him down here.'

'Ask *me*,' broke in a voice from the door, and Spooky Withers, in a very new and very flamboyant dressing-gown over equally new and flamboyant pyjamas, came into the room.

23

Mr. Withers's Business

He stood just within the doorway and surveyed them over the top of his pince-nez, looking rather like a dyspeptic schoolmaster who had been awakened to deal with a recalcitrant scholar.

'Good mornin', Spooky,' said Mr. Budd, eyeing him sleepily.

'What are you doing here, disturbing people from their sleep?' Withers demanded testily.

'Don't tell me you were asleep,' murmured Mr. Budd, shaking his head. 'I can't believe that, Spooky. I'll bet you've been very wide awake an' listenin' with both ears.'

'You'd lose your bet,' replied Spooky Withers. 'I heard what you said to Major Snodland just now because I couldn't help it. I've just come downstairs.'

'An' that's *all* you heard?' said the

detective sceptically.

'That's all. I should like — '

'A dreadful thing has happened, Withers,' broke in Snodland quickly. 'Mrs. Claydon has been murdered.'

Withers started and his long jaw dropped. It was very well done, but it did not deceive Mr. Budd for a moment. The lean man had known; in all probability had been listening for some time before he had made his rather dramatic entrance. 'Good heavens! How very terrible. When did it happen? Where . . . ?'

'It happened durin' the early hours of the mornin' in the ruins of the old abbey,' said Mr. Budd. 'An' Superintendent Boyder an' I are askin' Major Snodland a few questions.'

'Naturally — naturally,' said Withers. 'Dear me.' He clicked his teeth sorrowfully. 'How very, very dreadful. Poor lady. Who can have done such a terrible thing? Can there possibly be a maniac loose in the district?'

'I should think it very unlikely,' remarked Mr. Budd.

'Then how do you account for it?' said

Withers. 'Why should anyone wish to kill Mrs. Claydon? Such a charming and attractive woman. But perhaps you already have another suggestion?'

'Maybe I have,' answered Mr. Budd dryly. 'Without beatin' about the bush, Spooky, you're the only known person in the neighbourhood with a criminal record. S'pose you tell us what you're doin' here an' where you were durin' the night?'

'Me?' Mr. Withers looked the picture of righteous indignation. 'Surely you're not insinuating that I could've had anything to do with this — this horrible crime?'

'I'm askin' the questions an' I expect answers,' snapped Mr. Budd.

Withers turned to Major Snodland. 'You see,' he said sadly, 'this is what I've had to put up with for the last few years. Persecution, that's what it is, my dear sir, persecution.'

'Stick to the point,' snarled Mr. Budd; lack of sleep was making him cross. 'What brought you to Monk's Ferry?'

'I came at the request of Major Snodland, sir,' said Withers with great dignity. 'The major is very interested in psychical research, and invited me to come and stay with him and conduct several spiritualistic séances. We have, I'm glad to say, been remarkably successful in our contact with the spirit world.'

'Is this true?' Mr. Budd looked at Snodland, who nodded instantly.

'Perfectly true,' he said. 'I was going to tell you when Withers came in.'

'You know this man has been convicted twice for blackmail?'

'Yes, I know that. He told me himself. But it was a mistake.'

'It was nothin' of the sort,' said the detective. 'There are plenty o' people walkin' about who could tell you how much of a mistake it was. How did you get in touch with this man?'

'A friend of mine recommended him.'

'Hm,' muttered Mr. Budd, and then quickly: 'How was it, if you invited him down here, that you didn't recognize him when he came into The Monk's Head?'

'I didn't recognize him because I didn't know him then,' said Snodland.

'I was on my way here,' said Withers

smoothly. 'I only called into The Monk's Head for a drink after my journey from London. I didn't know Major Snodland, either.'

'Or Mrs. Claydon?' snapped Mr. Budd.

'Or Mrs. Claydon,' agreed Withers blandly.

It was all very slick and plausible — much too slick and plausible to be the truth. 'And what were you doin' durin' the night?' Mr. Budd demanded.

'I was in bed,' replied Withers. 'Isn't that right?' He appealed to Major Snodland for confirmation.

'That's right. Withers went up to bed as soon as we finished playing cards.'

'Before Mrs. Claydon went out?' asked Mr. Budd.

'Yes.'

Mr. Budd re-questioned them, but they stuck doggedly to their story and he couldn't shake it. 'I should like to have a look at the room occupied by Mrs. Claydon,' he said at last, yawning wearily.

Major Snodland offered no objection. He led the way upstairs and opened the door of a room in the front of the cottage.

It was low-ceilinged and not very large, but comfortably furnished. Several articles of clothing were scattered about, and two large suitcases stood at the foot of the bed. There was a subtle perfume in the air. The bed had not been slept in.

While Major Snodland stood in the doorway and watched him in silence, Mr. Budd made a careful examination of the room. He peered into the wardrobe, then opened the two suitcases and looked through their contents. On the dressing-table was a woman's handbag, and he examined that too. But he found nothing to help him. There were no letters or documents of any kind.

'Finished?' inquired Snodland with a slight sneer when Mr. Budd came to the end of his unprofitable search, and the detective nodded. They went downstairs, and very shortly afterward Mr. Budd and Boyder took their leave.

'You'll both be wanted at the inquest,' warned Mr. Budd as they went out. 'You'll be gettin' a subpoena in due course.'

Major Snodland watched them as far as

the gate and then closed the front door and turned to Withers, who was hovering behind him in the little hall. 'Thank God that's over,' he said fervently. 'Let's have a drink.' He went into the sitting-room, poured out two lavish whiskies, and handed one to Withers, who swallowed it eagerly.

'What do we do now?' he said.

Major Snodland put down his empty glass and shrugged. 'Sit tight and do nothing,' he replied. 'Confound it! Why did this have to happen? I was scared that that fellow would want to look at your room. *That* would have taken a lot of explaining away.'

'We'd better hide those things,' said Spooky Withers. 'I'll get them now.'

He hurried away up the stairs and presently returned with a grey bundle in his arms. It was the cowled habit of a monk.

★　★　★

Mr. Budd and Superintendent Boyder rejoined Gordon, and they all drove to

The Monk's Head. Mr. Jephcott was not up yet, but two of his daughters were, and they made coffee and brought it to the cheerless coffee-room. The three men were cold and tired, and the hot drinks both warmed and revived them.

'I'd like to know what those two are really up to,' said Boyder.

'So would I,' said Mr. Budd. 'That woman never went out in the pourin' rain to cure a headache, an' they know it. The question is, what *did* she go out for?'

'To keep an appointment, perhaps?' suggested Gordon.

'With the feller who killed her?' muttered Mr. Budd. 'That's unlikely. This feller was goin' ter spend the night searching Abbotsway for the Abbot's Key.'

'What's this, what's this?' broke in Boyder, looking in surprise from one to the other. 'What's the Abbot's Key?'

Mr. Budd sighed. Of course, Boyder knew nothing about the key or the theory he had formulated. It wouldn't do any harm to enlighten him, though his secretive nature flinched from the job.

Slowly he outlined his idea, and Boyder listened with increasing astonishment. When he had finished, the local superintendent whistled softly.

'You seem to have got it all worked out,' he said. 'So this old legend of the Twelve Apostles is at the bottom of the whole business, is it?'

'That's my opinion,' said Mr. Budd.

'You're probably right,' said Boyder thoughtfully, 'considering what this man Cator said before he died. Well, it'll be something to put before the chief constable.'

'No,' said Mr. Budd emphatically. 'I don't want it put before *anybody* at present. It's only a theory — there's nothin' to back it up — an' it's better if we keep it to ourselves.'

'But the chief constable . . . ' protested Boyder.

'Not even the chief constable,' said Mr. Budd. 'If it should 'appen to leak out, what we think, it would put this unknown feller on his guard at once, an' we'd never get him. At present he's no idea that we know anythin' about Lew Cator or suspect that this treasure's got anythin' to do with the murders. He'll go on tryin' to get it, an' that's how we're goin' to get *him*.'

Boyder realized that there was truth in what he said, and reluctantly agreed to keep it to himself.

'To go back to what I was sayin' before,' said Mr. Budd, 'about this woman Claydon keepin' an appointment with the man who killed 'er. You see where the snag comes in? If any such appointment had been made, it 'ud have been at Abbotsway, not the ruins.'

'Then what do you think happened?' asked Gordon.

'I don't know, Mr. Ashford. Maybe this woman went to the ruins for some purpose of her own an' saw somethin' she shouldn't have seen. That seems likely.'

'Do you think these people — Withers, Snodland, and Mrs. Claydon — are after the treasure, too?' put in Boyder.

'I wouldn't be surprised,' said Mr. Budd. 'There was some connection between Marie and the woman, I'm certain. Maybe I'll know more about it soon. I've asked for a check-up on the life of Snodland and Mrs. Claydon. It was Leek's idea, an' I'm waiting for the report from the Yard.' He paused and frowned. 'Talkin' of Leek,' he said seriously, 'I wonder where that feller can have got to? I'm beginnin' ter get a bit anxious.'

He got more anxious as the day went on, for there was no sign of the melancholy sergeant. Nor had he put in an appearance when darkness fell and night came down, wet and gloomy, on the village of Monk's Ferry.

24

What Happened to Leek

Leaning against the trunk of a tree that offered some slight protection from the wind, Sergeant Leek shivered and decided that life was very hard. He was being compelled to spend the greater part of the night in miserable discomfort, watching for something that never happened, and, he was convinced, never would happen. The whole thing was a waste of time. The people who lived in Abbot's Rest never did anything that was worth watching.

There was a light in the ground-floor window now; presently it would go out, and there would be a light in the upstairs window. Then that would go out. Was *that* worth keeping awake all night and freezing to death for?

A large drop began to form at the end of his thin nose, and he wiped it away with his handkerchief. If he got through this job without catching his death of cold, he'd be lucky. He pulled a thick woollen muffler closer round his throat and sank his chin into its comforting folds. Why was it, he thought, that he always got the worst jobs? He ought to have been promoted long ago. It was unfair that they should have overlooked him. Sheer favouritism, that's what it was. And there were younger men who hadn't been in the force as long as he, who were already inspectors. Something wrong with the whole system.

It began to rain — a few drops here and there at first, and then a steady downpour. The tree offered some protection, but not much, and before very long his shoulders were sopping and little streams of water were running off the brim of his hat. He cursed gently below his breath. Whatever happened, he'd got to stick it until five o'clock when his relief was due. The light in the window of Abbot's Rest still burned steadily. The inhabitants were staying up later than usual. Why anybody who had a chance of going to bed should prefer to stay up was more than he could understand.

Hello, what was happening over at the cottage? The door was opening and somebody was coming out. Leek peered through the semi-darkness. He could hear the whispering of voices, but not what they were saying. After a minute the voices ceased and the front door closed, but somebody was coming down the path — a woman, to judge by the footsteps. It must be Mrs. Rita Claydon. Where on earth could she be going on a night like this?

She came down the lane, passed close to where he was concealed, and turned into the Abbotsway road. Should he follow her, or should he remain and keep an eye on the cottage? Leek decided on the former option. Slipping out from the clump of trees, he followed the sound of her fading footsteps, keeping to the grass verge of the road himself so that his own footsteps were inaudible. He could see her, dimly, hurrying along through the rain, and decreased his pace so as not to get too close.

She kept straight on, following the

rough road, and at last it dawned on Leek that she must be going to either Abbotsway or the ruins of the old Abbey. The road frayed into open country beyond that.

She hurried along, her head bent to the rain, and apparently had no suspicion that she was being followed, for she never once looked back. Probably she thought it was unlikely that anyone would be abroad on such a night.

Now forgetful of his wet condition, Leek trailed along in the rear. As she drew near to Abbotsway, the moon came out, and the lean sergeant, realizing that should she look round he would be plainly visible, left the road and dodged into the fringe of the belt of woodland that skirted it. It was as well he did, for the woman ahead slowed down, stopped, and looked quickly about. Then instead of going on towards the house, she veered sharply and began to make her way to the ruins.

Leek stood in the cover of a tree-trunk and watched her. It was impossible to follow her now. Nothing could prevent him being seen; it was all open ground. He watched her receding figure growing smaller and wondered what to do next. If the moon would only go in he could risk it, but the moon stayed. He saw her disappear among the heaps of stones, and rubbed his wet face thoughtfully.

He wished fervently that he was near enough to see, but he dare not cross the open space in the moonlight. And then like the sudden extinguishing of a candle, the dim light vanished as the gathering clouds closed over the moon, and the whole scene went dark.

Leek left the fringe of the wood quickly and hurried towards the ruins, hoping that the darkness would remain to cover his approach. As he neared them he slowed down and proceeded more cautiously. He reached a great pile of stones and stopped to listen, but he could hear nothing. Moving forward carefully, he found himself inside the ruins, but there was no sign of Rita Claydon. An acrid smell drifted past his nostrils, and as he recognized the herblike scent of incense his heart gave a leap. The sudden chill of fear gripped him, and he gasped to recover his breath and found that he was shaking. But he mastered the panic, which made him want to turn and run, and went stealthily forward.

He heard a sound now — a queer, chanting sound that made the hair on his neck rise stiffly, and then a figure loomed up from behind a heap of broken masonry. He caught a glimpse of a long robe and a cowled head, and cried out sharply — and then the great arch above him seemed to collapse on his head, and everything went black . . .

★　★　★

Sergeant Leek heard faintly, and as though from far away, the sound of someone moaning. He opened his eyes and discovered that it was himself. He was lying in a vaulted chamber of stone, the groined roof supported by squat stone pillars. He thought at first that it was a church, but the roof was too low for that.

It was a vast place full of shadows, which an oil lamp hanging from a great rusty hook did little to dispel. At one end was an archway with a flight of worn stone steps beyond leading upward. That was all he saw, for his head pained so violently that he was forced to close his eyes. But he could smell incense strongly — the place was full of it.

He must have lapsed into a semi-coma again, for when he opened his eyes for the second time he was being watched by a small, wizened man whose face was vaguely familiar.

'So yer've come rahned, 'ave yer?' said the man in broad Cockney, his little beady eyes moving restlessly. 'Cripes, I was beginnin' ter think yer was a gawner.'

'What is this place?' asked Leek weakly.

'This is me country seat,' answered the little man with a wide grin, displaying a mouth full of broken yellow teeth. 'Nice place, ain't it?'

'Was it you who coshed me?'

'No, it weren't me. I didn't 'ave nuthin' to do with it. If we go on at this rate, we shall be gettin' full up,' he remarked cryptically.

'I know you,' said Leek suddenly. 'Your

name's Sam Lisker. You've been inside.'

'That's right — seven convictions,' said Sam Lisker proudly.

'Looks as though you'll be gettin' another,' grunted Leek.

'Not me! I'm goin' ter be rich — rollin' in spondulicks — that'll be me.'

'Bashin' officers of the law is a serious offence,' said the sergeant severely. 'They'll give yer a heavy sentence fer that.'

'I tell yer I didn't bash yer. It was 'im what did that.'

'Who's 'him'?'

'The bloke what's goin' to make me rich,' Sam said, and he looked about uneasily. ''E brought me 'ere — ter this place. I 'ad to 'elp 'im git the gal.'

'Miss Shannon?' said Leek quickly. 'Is she here?'

'Through there.' Sam jerked his head towards a heavy oak door on one side of the vaulted chamber, which Leek had not noticed before. 'She 'asn't been 'urt,' he added hastily. 'She's got plenty o' rugs, an' a portable wireless, an' 'eaps an 'eaps o' food. There's a great stack o' tinned

271

stuff down 'ere — 'nough fer a blinkin' regiment.' He broke off suddenly. 'I'm talkin' too much,' he muttered. 'If 'e 'eard me, I wouldn't 'alf cop it.' He was clearly scared to death of the person he referred to as ' ''im'.

'You'll cop it anyway,' said Leek. 'You're goin' to be in bad trouble, Lisker. This feller you keep talkin' about is wanted fer the Big Thing, an' you've made yourself an assess'ry. You know what that means.'

'I couldn't 'elp it — I 'ad ter do wot 'e told me. 'E's a devil.' He stopped abruptly and listened. ''Ere 'e comes now,' he whispered. There was a faint scraping sound and then a footfall on stone. A tall figure appeared on the stairway beyond the arch and came hurriedly into the vault. It wore the cowled habit of a monk and was breathing hard.

'Wot's up?' said Sam in alarm. 'I didn't think you was comin' back yet.'

'There was somebody in the house,' panted the newcomer in a muffled voice. 'I nearly walked into them. I had to run

272

for it.' He leaned against one of the squat pillars and tried to recover his breath. Leek saw that under the cowl something dark had been tied over the man's face.

'What's this infernal smell that's filling the place?' asked the cowled man suddenly. 'I could smell it outside. It's like a church.'

Sam Lisker moved uneasily. 'It's my fault, guv'nor,' he muttered. 'I chucked away a fag end an' it fell in a heap of dark stuff in a corner by those steps, an' the stuff started to smoulder.'

The other uttered an angry exclamation, and then he chuckled. 'Oh well,' he said. 'Perhaps it was a lucky accident. If anybody comes near the ruins and smells incense, they'll probably run like the devil.'

So, thought Leek, *this place is under the old abbey, is it?*

'There's quite a lot of the stuff,' said Sam. 'A dirty, brownish sort o' powder.'

'Where the old monks emptied their censers, I expect.' The cowled man had recovered his breath, and now he walked over and looked down at Leek. 'Come round, have you?' he said. 'What were you doing snooping round the ruins? Did you come with the Claydon woman?'

The lean sergeant said nothing.

'Not talking, eh?' muttered the unknown. 'Well, it doesn't matter.' He turned to Lisker. 'How's the woman?'

'She's awlright. She's 'ad a good feed, an' she's been listenin' to the wireless. A blinkin' awful programme, too — a church choir or sump'n. She seemed ter like it. Gimme Tommy 'Andley any day.'

The cowled man was apparently paying little attention to what he said, for he suddenly broke in: 'This'll mean an alteration in my plans. If the police are going to keep a watch in Abbotsway, all the trouble we went to over the woman is going to be useless. I shall have to think of something else. I'd better go now if the coast's clear. Keep an eye on that fellow.'

'What are yer goin' ter do with 'im?' asked Lisker.

'I don't know yet. He may prove useful — that's why I brought him here. If he doesn't . . . ' He shrugged his shoulders. 'We can always dump his body in the ruins and make another murder mystery out of him.'

He went quickly to the archway and up the stairs. There was a long pause and then a dull thud. Sam heaved a sigh and turned, his wrinkled face a curious yellowish-grey.

'Who is 'e?' asked Leek.

'What I told yer,' answered Sam Lisker huskily. 'A devil.'

25

The Man who Came

If the murder of Lloyd Gibbs and the disappearance of Eileen Shannon had caused a sensation in Monk's Ferry, it was nothing compared to the sensation caused by the murder of Mrs. Rita Claydon. It created something that was akin to a panic. Terror reared its stark and ugly head, and the bar at The Monk's Head reflected the general feeling of the village by being conspicuously empty on the evening following the discovery of the woman's body in the ruins.

Peter Walton spent the day telephoning long and vivid accounts to a delighted news editor, openly declaring that Monk's Ferry was the answer to a reporter's prayer. Mr. Budd was less jubilant, wandering about with a furrowed brow and a look of unusual gloom on his florid face.

He was worried about many things,

chief among which was the continued absence of Leek. In the afternoon he went reluctantly over to Barnford to attend a conference presided over by the chief constable. That rather irascible gentleman was particularly trying. The weary Mr. Budd and the almost equally weary Superintendent Boyder had all their work cut out to satisfy his curiosity without giving too much away.

The meeting culminated in a long speech by the chief constable which boiled down to plain honest-to-God English, merely reiterating that 'something must be done at once'. Since both Mr. Budd and Boyder were perfectly aware of this, and each was doing all that was possible, the chief constable's eloquence was a trifle redundant.

The detective came back to Monk's Ferry and, dodging Peter Walton, who had been looking for him for the greater part of the afternoon, locked himself in his room at the inn and sat down to write a long and laborious report to his immediate chief at Scotland Yard. It occupied him for nearly three hours; and when he had finished it he read it through, nodded to himself with approval, and, putting it in an envelope, licked down the flap, addressed it, and put it in his pocket ready for posting.

Going down to dinner, he found Peter Walton in the coffee-room and accepted the fact with a sigh of resignation. The reporter got up and came and sat at his table.

'Ah,' he said cheerfully, 'at last we're alone! Now what do you mean by this game of hide-and-seek? I've been trying to get hold of you all day.'

Mr. Budd unfolded his napkin and tucked it beneath his chin. 'I've got somethin' better to do than answer a lot o' questions.' He leaned back in his chair and looked at the ceiling. 'Much as it may surprise you to hear, there's quite a lot of routine work attachin' to wilful murder, an' I've been very busy.'

'So have I,' said Peter. 'I've broken the record of the original busy bee today, and old 'May Blossom'' — he referred to the taciturn and disillusioned Mr. Hawthorne, the news editor — 'is going wild with excitement. Every time they tell him it's me on the phone, he does a jitterbug round the office.'

'I wonder he don't shoot himself,' snarled Mr. Budd unkindly. 'Why can't you eat yer dinner an' shut up?'

'I'll shut up if you'll talk,' answered Peter calmly. 'After all the suggestions I've offered you, is it fair to treat me like this?'

'The only suggestions you've made to me have been bad 'uns. You thought Michael Shannon killed Gibbs . . . ' He snorted derisively.

'I made a mistake,' said Peter with disarming candour. 'I must have, since he couldn't have been responsible for this other murder. But at least I told you what I thought and what I'd found out. I don't keep things to myself like you do.'

'How do you know I keep things to myself?' said Mr. Budd.

'What about last night? Do you call it a friendly act to go sneaking off on your own to Abbotsway? You might at least have let me in on it.'

'So that you could phone the *Post-Courier*, I s'pose?' growled Mr. Budd sarcastically. 'I don't want everything I do blazoned forth on the front page o' that rag o' yours.'

'The *Post-Courier* is a very respectable and widely read newspaper,' said Peter solemnly. 'Its proprietor is a shining light in the House of Lords — a highly respected peer of the realm.'

'I s'pose 'e does a jitterbug, too, every time you ring up,' grunted Mr. Budd, 'round the House o' Lords.' He began to drink the soup which one of Mr. Jephcott's daughters had set before him.

Peter, who had already dined, listened to this rather noisy operation for a moment in silence. Then he said seriously: 'Joking apart, Budd, why *did* you go to Abbotsway last night?'

'How did you know I went there?'

'Common sense and deduction. You discovered the murder in the early hours of the morning — ergo, you must've been somewhere near the ruins. Colonel Shannon and his family left in the afternoon and Abbotsway was empty — ergo again, you were probably at Abbotsway. Question: What did you go there for?'

Mr. Budd pushed aside his empty soup plate and looked at Peter sleepily while he crumbled his bread. 'I wouldn't call that deduction,' he murmured, shaking his head. 'I'd call it guessin'.'

'Was it a good guess?' demanded Peter with a grin.

'Pretty fair,' said Mr. Budd, inspecting the plate of roast lamb that arrived at that moment.

'Well, what was the idea, then?' said the reporter impatiently. 'What did you expect to find in an empty house?'

'Emptiness!' retorted Mr. Budd, and he shook his head again. 'It's no good, Walton. I'm not talkin'.' He helped himself to vegetables with great care.

'You're the most exasperating man I've ever met,' Peter declared.

'You should meet the chief constable,' grunted Mr. Budd. 'Maybe you'd change your opinion.' He went on with his dinner, and no amount of questioning could make him say any more.

'You're impossible,' Peter grumbled irritably. 'You might at least give me some idea of the line on which you're working.'

'I might, but what I'm workin' on is more like a railway junction than a line. The points is all mixed up, an' there's nobody in the signal-box to straighten 'em out. Maybe when I find which line's goin' ter take me to the right platform, I'll tell you.'

Peter left him alone and he calmly finished his dinner, smoked a cigar, and then went and telephoned the police station. Fowler, in answer to his inquiry, informed him that there was still no news of Leek, and the detective went into the bar, filled with anxiety. It began to look as if something serious had happened to the melancholy sergeant, and he decided that if he had not turned up by the morning he would arrange with Boyder for a search-party to comb the district.

The bar was almost entirely empty. Fear had kept the majority of the villagers in their own homes that night. According to Mr. Jephcott, the village was split up into two camps — those who believed that the murders were the result of supernatural forces, and those who believed that a dangerous lunatic was at large, killing for the sheer lust of blood. But whichever belief they held, nobody was anxious to be abroad after dusk.

Mr. Budd drank his beer gloomily and had another with Peter Walton, who joined him later. Then, going to his room, he changed his blue serge for a worn tweed, put on his heavy overcoat and set out for Abbotsway. He had arranged to meet Gordon at the back gate at ten o'clock. It was a dark night, and although it was not actually raining, the air was damp and chill.

Gordon was waiting for him at the appointed place and they walked through the sodden garden towards the house. It was very quiet. The wind had almost entirely dropped, and the trees were motionless. They negotiated the small window once more and crept through to the hall. The old house was completely still. Not a creak or a crack disturbed the heavy silence. Even the clock had run down. Gordon Ashford looked around in the dim light of Mr. Budd's torch and sat down on the chair he had occupied the previous night. 'Do you suppose this man will come again?' he whispered.

'I don't know,' answered Mr. Budd softly. 'We can't afford to take any chances, though.'

'If he comes, he'll be taking an appalling risk.'

Mr. Budd shrugged. 'I've known people take bigger risks for a million quid,' he answered. 'Maybe he won't come tonight, or tomorrow night, or the night after, but he'll come one night, an' that's the night we'll get him.'

They sat in the dark and the minutes dragged slowly by. It was extraordinary, thought Gordon, how he missed the friendly tick-tock of the big clock. The house seemed somehow dead without it, as though its heart had stopped beating. The stillness began to act on him like a soporific, and his head sank gently forward until his chin was resting on his chest. His breathing became slower and more regular . . .

Mr. Budd, tired from his wakeful night and busy day, nodded too, and the ghost of an unmusical snore drifted through the silence.

Eleven o'clock . . . twelve . . .

The detective woke suddenly with a start and a faint sound in his ears that he could not place. Sitting up, he peered into the surrounding blackness and listened. There was a stealthy movement — and it came from *inside* the house.

Mr. Budd, alert and thoroughly wakeful, slid a hand into the pocket of his coat and withdrew the automatic pistol. With his thumb he pressed down the safety-catch and waited. There came to his ears the faint creak of a door, and then the sound of a cautious footstep. It was barely audible, but there was no mistake. Somebody was creeping along the passage from the back of the house towards the hall.

Mr. Budd's body stiffened. One hand gripped the pistol and the other held his torch ready — waiting for the moment when those stealthy steps should reach the hall. They came on, unevenly, as though the person who made them groped his way in the dark, and then they reached the hall.

Mr. Budd came to his feet and pressed

the button of the torch in one concerted movement. The ray, sweeping forward through the darkness, focused on a crouching figure at the entrance to the passage.

'Keep still an' put yer hands up!' ordered Mr. Budd sharply. 'I've got a gun an' I'll shoot if you move.'

'So this is how you spend your evenings?' said a familiar voice. 'You be careful with that thing, Budd, it might go off.'

Mr. Budd uttered an unprintable exclamation. It was Peter Walton!

26

The Tapping in the Cellar

Peter surveyed him coolly, an impudent grin on his freckled face. 'You can't get away with it twice,' he said. 'I saw you leave the inn and I guessed you were coming here. I thought I might as well join the happy party.'

Mr. Budd slipped the pistol back in his pocket and glared angrily at the reporter. 'I oughter arrest you for interferin' with the police in the execution of their duty,' he growled severely. 'Do you realize that by comin' here like this you may have spoiled everythin'?'

'Spoiled what?'

'Never mind what,' snarled Mr. Budd. 'Just you keep quiet now you *are* here.'

'I wish you wouldn't be so damned secretive. I could help.'

'I don't want you to help. All I want yer ter do is shut up! You've done enough damage already, an' I don't want you ter do any more.'

Peter sat down at the foot of the stairs. 'I'll shut up. But now I'm here, I'm going to stay. If anything happens, I'm going to be in on it.'

Mr. Budd muttered something that was distinctly uncomplimentary and lowered himself carefully back into his chair.

It was pretty certain that the unknown man who was so anxious to get possession of the Abbot's Key would be watching, and if he saw anyone in the vicinity of the old house it would scare him off. Mr. Budd felt that his annoyance was justified. There was nothing that could be done about it, however. All he could do was to wait for the morning and hope for the best.

With infinite slowness the long night passed. But nothing happened. Towards morning it began to rain. They heard it pattering on the shrubs outside, and presently a faint grey light began to show at the windows. It grew lighter, and Mr. Budd eased his cramped limbs and looked at his watch. It was getting on for half-past seven. With a yawn he stood up and stretched himself, waking Gordon, who had dropped off again into an uneasy doze.

'We may as well give it up,' grunted the superintendent wearily. 'He won't come now.'

'Who won't come?' said Peter. 'Who are you waiting for?'

'Father Christmas,' growled Mr. Budd. 'Come on, we'll be gettin' back. I want lots o' hot coffee an' some breakfast . . . ' He stopped. From somewhere beneath them came a faint sound of tapping — a muffled sound like stone against stone. 'What was that? Did you hear it?'

Gordon nodded. 'It sounded as if it was somewhere below.'

'Water in the pipes?' suggested Peter practically, but Mr. Budd wasn't listening. He had gone over to the passage leading to the kitchen. They followed him through into the big old-fashioned scullery until he paused before a heavy worm-eaten oaken door.

'This must lead down to the cellars,' muttered Mr. Budd, almost to himself.

'We forgot the cellars last night, Ashford.'

Peter Walton shot them a curious glance, but for once he said nothing, mastering his curiosity with an obvious effort. Mr. Budd tried the wrought-iron handle of the door, but it refused to open. 'Locked,' he grunted briefly.

'That key . . . on the mantelpiece in the kitchen . . . ' began Gordon.

'Maybe,' said Mr. Budd. 'Get it, will you?'

Gordon hurried away, coming back almost at once with a key which the big man took from him and fitted into the lock. It turned easily and the door came open. Beyond, a flight of worn stone steps led downwards into darkness. Mr. Budd peered about inside the door, found a light switch and pressed it down.

A light came on below, and at almost the same instant the muffled tapping, which had ceased, began again. There was no doubt now that it originated from somewhere in the cellar.

They all three descended the steps and found themselves in a huge underground chamber that apparently extended under the entire house. It was very clean and tidy, and had obviously been used both as a storeroom and a wine cellar. In wooden racks, built against the stone walls, were scores of ancient bottles, dusty and cobwebbed. The wood of the racks was old and worm-eaten and must have been as ancient as the house itself.

'Some wine cellar,' said Peter, staring about. 'Old Shannon did himself pretty well.'

The tapping came from a corner, behind a rack of port, and Mr. Budd went over and frowned at the place whence it came. 'There's somebody behind the wall,' he grunted. 'That tappin's muffled, but it's clear enough. There's somebody bangin' on the other side of that wall with a brick or sump'n.'

The knocking ceased abruptly, and there was silence, and then another sound reached them — a queer rumbling sound, accompanied by the grinding squeak of metal.

'Look,' breathed Gordon. 'Look . . . '

The racks of wine bottles were moving towards them, slowly and steadily, and with them came the solid wall of stone. A section was swinging outward like a door. Further and further it moved, and then through the black opening came a staggering form smothered in dust and dirt and cobwebs — a lean figure, dishevelled and panting.

'Leek!' exclaimed Mr. Budd in complete astonishment. 'Where the devil 'ave you come from . . . ?'

'Get me out of that awful place,' croaked the voice of the sergeant hoarsely. 'For Gawd's sake get me out! It's full o' dead men . . . '

They took the unfortunate Leek up to the scullery and sat him down in a chair and gave him water, which he drank thirstily, washing away the dust that had clogged his mouth and throat and half-choked him.

'Now then,' said Mr. Budd when he had partially recovered, 'let's hear all about it. What's all this about the place bein' full o' dead men?'

'There's scores of 'em,' said Leek with a shudder, 'bursting out of rottin' coffins . . . '

'How did you get down there?' demanded his superior, and the sergeant related his adventures of the previous night. When he mentioned Sam Lisker, Mr. Budd uttered an exclamation. 'So *he's* in it, is he,' he said.

'He's lookin' after the woman,' said Leek. 'She's — '

'Which woman? Do you mean Eileen?' broke in Gordon eagerly. 'Is she there?'

'Yes,' croaked the sergeant. 'In a — '

'Hi! Come back!' cried Mr. Budd as Ashford almost ran over to the cellar door. 'You just wait a bit, young feller.'

'I'm going to find Eileen,' said Gordon determinedly.

'You'll wait and go with us,' growled the superintendent. 'You're not goin' runnin' off on your own. Miss Shannon can wait for another half-hour or so.'

'But . . . ' began Ashford, but Mr. Budd interrupted him before he could go on.

'There ain't no 'buts',' he said stubbornly. 'We'll go an' have a look at this place in a minute an' get her out. Just hold on for a bit.'

Rather reluctantly, Gordon came back.

'Now,' continued Mr. Budd, 'let's have the rest of it, Leek, an' make it short.'

The sergeant complied, continuing from where he had left off.

'Any idea who this feller in the cowl was?' asked the superintendent when Leek reached that point in his story.

The sergeant shook his head. 'No, an' I don't think Lisker 'as either. When 'e went out for a breather, I managed to wriggle out o' the cords they'd tied me up with an' — '

'You can cut all that,' broke in Mr. Budd impatiently. 'You can tell us all about that later on. At present I want ter have a look at this place beyond the wine cellar. Come on.'

With a sigh, the weary Leek got up and they all went back to the cellar. The stone door was still open, and, led by the sergeant, they stepped gingerly into the darkness beyond.

'You got to be careful,' warned Leek. 'The ground's full of rubbish and stuff that's dropped from the roof. Further on you can only crawl, it's so narrow.'

Mr. Budd switched on his torch and

swept the light round. The passage was small and narrow, with an arched roof that had fallen in many places, showing the raw earth. Damp trickled down the sides and ugly-looking fungoid growths sprang from between the blocks of stone. The floor was littered with heaps of masonry over which they had to pick their way.

The passage dipped steeply and ran straight for about fifty yards, then twisted sharply to the left. After this turn it narrowed. There was so much rubbish, and the roof had sagged so dangerously, that they were forced to crawl for a good part of the way on their hands and knees — a difficult and unpleasant operation, especially for Mr. Budd, whose bulk was a great handicap. With a great deal of puffing and panting, however, he managed it; but when the tunnel widened and heightened, he stood up with a breath of relief.

'I thought we was never comin' to the end o' that,' he whispered breathlessly. 'That must be where it passes under the bed of the old river. Phew! I'm glad we don't 'ave ter go back the same way.'

'Do you good,' said Peter with a grin. 'Get your weight down. By Jove! If I could print this, the circulation would go up sky high.'

'If you print a word,' grunted Mr. Budd, 'somethin' 'ull go up sky high, an' it won't be the circulation! Where's all these dead men you was talkin' about?' he added to Leek.

'Further on,' said the sergeant. 'The place widens into a kind o' crypt, an' the coffins is there — piled one on the top o' the other, they are, and all rotten, with skeletons fallin' out of 'em.'

'Must've been a sort o' burial place for the old monks, I suppose,' remarked Mr. Budd, but Gordon Ashford corrected him.

'I don't think it could be,' he said doubtfully. 'There's a special place in the churchyard that used to be their burial ground.'

'Maybe it got too full,' said Mr. Budd, 'an' they used this for the overflow. Let's get on.'

There was very little more of the

passage, for which they were all thankful. As Leek had described, it suddenly emerged into a large oblong chamber like a crypt, which was full of rubble, fallen masonry, and a number of rotting wooden coffins, from the gaping sides of which bones protruded. It was a gruesome place enough, and looking round, there seemed to be no way out of it except by the tunnel along which they had come. But Leek soon showed them that there was. Going over to an apparently solid wall of stone, the sergeant thrust his fingers between a gap in the blocks and pulled. There was a grinding rumbling, similar to that which they had heard in the wine cellar at Abbotsway, and a portion of the wall began to open inwards. It moved slowly, a huge mass of masonry nearly two feet thick, and pivoted in the centre. They peered through into the great vaulted chamber where Leek had recovered consciousness.

'I found this by accident while I was searchin' about,' explained the sergeant. 'You open it the same way on this side as you do on the other. It looks 'eavy, but it moves easy.' He pulled the stone and it swung to and shut with a click.

'Must be a perfect balance,' said Peter. 'It's surprising.'

'Never mind that,' broke in Gordon, who had been in a fever of impatience all through the journey. 'Where's Eileen?'

Leek pointed to the arched door in the wall. 'Lisker said she was in there.'

Almost before the words had left his lips, Ashford was at the door and tugging at the rusty wrought-iron handle. 'It's locked,' he panted disgustedly.

'O' course it is, what did you expect?' retorted Mr. Budd. 'But it won't be for long. Where's this feller, Lisker?'

'I don't know,' said Leek, shaking his head. ''E went out.'

'There's his bed, I should think,' put in Peter. He pointed to a mattress and some blankets between two of the squat pillars.

'If he's out, we'll wait fer 'im ter come back,' said Mr. Budd. 'He'll have the key ter that door.'

'Listen,' said Gordon suddenly. 'What's that?'

There was a scraping noise from the stairway beyond the arch.

'That's Lisker,' whispered Leek. 'There was a — '

'Shh,' snapped Mr. Budd as there came a faint thud followed by a quick footstep.

Mr. Lisker came hastily down the stone steps, took two paces into the vault, and stopped dead. His mouth gaped and his eyebrows shot upwards so that his little wrinkled face looked like a coconut at a fair. ''Ere,' he gasped, 'what's all this? 'Ow did you all get in 'ere?'

'That doesn't matter, Sam,' said Mr. Budd. 'The point is that we *are* here, an' your little game's up.'

'Blimey!' muttered the still-bewildered Lisker, ''Ow did you git in 'ere? Did 'e bring yer 'ere?'

'Who, Sam?' asked the superintendent kindly. He had known Sam Lisker for many years — had been in fact responsible for his first conviction — and he knew that the little crook suffered from a weak intellect. Sam Lisker was more to be pitied than blamed.

The little man looked about uneasily.

"Im,' he whispered. 'That devil.'

'No, Sam,' said Mr. Budd. 'We came on our own. What's this feller's name?'

'I don't know 'is name,' said Sam, shaking his head, 'but 'e's goin' ter make me a rich man. Thousands an' thousands o' quid, I'm goin' ter 'ave.'

'Now isn't that fine,' said Mr. Budd. 'Well, well! Goin' ter have lots o' money, are you, Sam? An' how's this feller goin' ter get hold of all this money ter give yer, Sam?'

'I dunno. That's a secret. But 'e'll do it. 'E's a clever bloke, 'e is, an' a devil.'

'Never mind him, Sam,' said Mr. Budd. 'You got the key to this door?'

'I've got it, but you can't 'ave it. 'E'd kill me if I give it ter yer.'

'He won't get a chance,' said the detective. 'You'll be coming along with us, an' so will the young lady you've got in that room. So be a good feller, Sam, an' hand over the key.' He held out his hand, but the little man shrank away.

'No, I can't. 'E'd kill me,' he whispered, 'an' I wouldn't git the money.'

'You wouldn't get it, anyway. He's been

foolin' you, Sam. You wouldn't get any money. When he's finished with you all you'll get is a knife in yer back, or a cosh on the head.'

A look of fear came into the beady eyes. 'Yes, 'e'd do it. E's a devil, 'e is.' He considered, his small face crinkled up like a walnut. 'If I gives yer the key,' he said after a pause, 'will you promise you'll keep '*im* away from me?'

'I promise you that, Sam,' Mr. Budd said, and Sam Lisker gave him the key.

27

A Report from the Yard

Mr. Budd went straight over to the oak door, and, twisting the key in the lock, opened it. Beyond was a small cell-like room of stone, lighted dimly by an oil lamp that stood on the bare floor. The woman who was asleep on a mattress in one corner, covered with blankets, started up with a startled cry as they came in.

'Eileen!' Gordon ran over to her and, dropping on his knees, put an arm round her shoulders.

'Gordon?' She looked sleepily at him, her eyes dazed and bewildered. 'What's happened? How ... how did you get here?'

'We've come to take you home, miss,' said Mr. Budd gently. 'If you're feelin' strong enough.'

'I'm quite all right,' she said quickly. 'That funny little man was very kind. I've

302

had plenty of food.' She pushed back the blankets and got up. She was dressed in the tweed suit that had been taken from her wardrobe. 'I must look a dreadful sight,' she said ruefully. 'I haven't been able to wash.'

'You look lovely!' said Gordon fervently, and Mr. Budd thought that this was a slight exaggeration, since Eileen Shannon's face was streaked with grime and her hair resembled a bird's nest in a gale of wind.

'You'll have to let us take you to The Monk's Head,' said the detective. 'Your family are away.'

'I'll take her home,' declared Gordon firmly. 'Mother will look after her.'

'Why have they gone away?' asked Eileen in surprise.

'I dare say your father'll explain, miss,' answered Mr. Budd. 'I expect as soon as 'e knows you've been found, 'e'll come back. I think Mr. Ashford's idea's a good one, so I'm goin' ter suggest that you go along with him now.'

'Yes, come on, Eileen,' said Gordon, who, now that she had been found, seemed to have no further interest in the proceedings. 'Never mind what you look like,' he added as she started to protest. 'You can put that right when you get to the farm.'

'We'd better get Sam to show us the way out,' murmured Mr. Budd. 'Hi, Sam! How d'we get out o' this place?'

Sam Lisker, still rather scared and uneasy, took them over to the steps and led the way up. They narrowed after a little way, and just at the point where they did so, there was a deep niche in the stone wall in which hung a grey garment. Mr. Budd peered at it as they went by. It was a monk's habit and cowl, and there were dull, rusty stains on the rough cloth.

'The butcher's overall,' he muttered under his breath to Peter, and the reporter nodded. 'Maybe we'll find his knife, too.'

The steps were so narrow higher up that there was only room for one person at a time. Sam Lisker went first and the others followed. At the top was a little platform and a curved wall. Lisker put his fingers into a narrow slit, as Leek had done, and, with the now-familiar grinding sound, the curved wall moved outwards. They passed through the small aperture and found themselves in the ruins of Felsbank Abbey. A portion of the base of the truncated tower stood ajar, like a door. Lisker swung it shut and there was nothing to be seen. It fitted perfectly and blended so well with the other stonework that, even if anyone had known it was there, they would have had difficulty in finding it.

'You'd never guess, would you?' murmured Mr. Budd admiringly. 'Them monks an' abbots were clever old fellers. The steps must be built in the thickness o' the wall.'

'What a story!' breathed Peter.

'How d'you open it from this side, Sam?' asked Mr. Budd, and Lisker showed him — a heavy pressure on a certain stone, and slowly the door swung open again.

'Like a bit out o' the Forty Thieves an' Ali Baba,' said Leek. 'I remember when I was a boy they took me ter see — '

'We haven't time to listen to your life story now,' broke in Mr. Budd. 'You take the young lady home with you, Mr. Ashford, an' I'll notify her father that she's been found.'

Gordon slipped his hand under Eileen's arm. 'Come along,' he said, 'we'll just be in time for breakfast.'

'What I want is a hot bath,' she answered.

They said goodbye to Mr. Budd and the others and set off for Long Meadow Farm. Peter looked after them curiously. 'How long has *that* been going on?' he asked.

'Quite a while,' said Mr. Budd with a slight twinkle in his eyes. 'Old Shannon rather objected by all accounts. Maybe he'll be a bit more reasonable now. Ashford's a nice young feller.'

'How did you get to be so friendly with him?'

'You'd be surprised how friendly I get with all sorts o' people. I'm naturally of a friendly disposition. Come on, we'll have another look inside here.'

They went back through the stone door, and Mr. Budd descended the steps until he came to the niche in which the monk's habit hung. Taking it down, he examined it, frowning heavily. After a minute or so he thrust a gloved hand inside the robe and brought out a long knife, the blade of which was sheathed in leather.

'Here's the murderer's weapon,' he remarked, handling the gruesome thing gingerly. 'I'll have it tested for prints, though I don't suppose I'll be lucky. He's almost certain to have worn gloves.' He put the knife away in his breast pocket after wrapping it up carefully in a clean handkerchief, and stared thoughtfully at the grey robe.

'This is new,' he murmured, 'an' the maker's name's been cut out, but we may be able to trace it. These stains are blood, I think. Some of 'em are fresh, too. That'll be from Mrs. Claydon. He came here an' put on his disguise, did what he had to do, an' took it off before he left. Hm, I've got an idea that it was while he was comin' or goin' that he bumped into Lloyd Gibbs.'

Peter stared with fascinated eyes at the stained garment and gave a little shudder.

'I wonder who he is,' he muttered.

''E's a devil, that's who 'e is,' cried Sam Lisker, who was hovering uneasily at his elbow. 'You get me away from 'ere before 'e comes.'

'All right, Sam, all right,' said Mr. Budd soothingly. 'We'll take you back with us, don't you worry. I'll have a watch put on this place day an' night,' he added to Peter, 'in case this feller does come again.'

'Have you any idea who he is?' asked the reporter.

The detective nodded. 'I know one of his names. At least, I think I do — Jackson.'

'Jackson?' repeated Peter, wrinkling his forehead. 'Who's he?'

'He's the King Pippin,' said Mr. Budd. 'He's the feller responsible fer all this.'

The reporter looked at him curiously. 'How did you find all this out?' I said you'd got something up your sleeve . . . '

'I found it out by usin' me brains. Jest puttin' two an' two tergether an' makin' 'em add up to four. Well, we can't waste any more time here talkin'. You take that feller back to Fowler's cottage, Leek,' he went on, turning to the sergeant. 'Go with him, Sam. He'll take care of you.'

'Ain't you comin'?' said Lisker. 'If that devil finds I've gone, he'll come after me.'

'No, no, he won't,' said Mr. Budd. 'Now don't you go worryin' any more. Go along with Sergeant Leek like a good feller, an' I'll come an' see you later.'

Mr. Lisker was only partially reassured. He looked hesitantly and rather dubiously from the superintendent to Leek, and the frightened expression did not leave his beady eyes.

'Come along,' said the sergeant, pulling him gently by the arm. 'You'll be all right.'

With repeated glances over his shoulder, the little man allowed himself to be led away. When he had gone, Mr. Budd turned to Peter Walton and made a grimace.

'Poor little feller, he's scared stiff,' he said. 'Got the mind of a child of ten. His mother drank herself to death before he was three, an' his father died in an asylum. Didn't give 'im much chance, did it?'

'Do you think he knows anything about

this man we're after?' asked the reporter.

Mr. Budd shook his head. 'No, nuthin' of any use. I don't s'pose he ever saw his face — Jackson 'ud be too clever for that. Sam might remember somethin' about him that 'ud be useful, but I'm a bit doubtful.' He yawned wearily and looked about. 'I think we'll close this place up an' get along back to the pub. Later on I'd like to have a good look over it, but not now.'

'Murders, secret passages, abductions,' said Peter ecstatically. 'Everything the heart of the great British public could desire, and a news editor dreams about. Can't I just telephone — '

'You can telephone nuthin',' said Mr. Budd curtly. 'Not one single word about this until I give yer permission.'

'And when will that be?'

'When I introduce you to Jackson. When I do that, you'll have a story that'll be worth waitin' for. Let's get goin'.'

They reached The Monk's Head to find Boyder waiting. He had just driven over from Barnford and had arrived a few seconds before them. 'Well this beats everything I've ever heard,' he exclaimed when Mr. Budd acquainted him with what had happened. 'A secret passage from the old ruins to Abbotsway? Who'd've thought it?' He shook his head. 'And Miss Shannon was there all the time? We'll have to let the colonel know she's been found.'

'There's a lot o' things we'll have ter do,' said Mr. Budd, 'and one of the first is to get hold of two of your men to keep watch on that place in case this feller turns up. I don't think he will, but he might.'

'I'll attend to that,' said Boyder. 'Is there a telephone hereabouts?'

Mr. Budd directed him to the instrument and hurried away. While he was gone, Mr. Jephcott appeared with a bulky, official-looking envelope. 'Just come by post,' he said, giving it to Mr. Budd. 'It was registered and I signed for it.'

'Thank you,' murmured the detective. He took the envelope and gazed at it for a moment in sleepy rumination. Then inserted a thumb under the flap and tore it open. There were several sheets of paper covered with type, and he examined them swiftly while Peter looked on, obviously bursting with curiosity to know what they were.

'Hm. Well, that's that!' grunted Mr. Budd noncommittally as he thrust them back in the envelope and put it in his pocket. 'Things is lookin' up.'

'What's the news?' demanded Peter, unable to contain himself any longer. 'What was in that?'

'Just a few items concernin' our friend Major Snodland,' murmured Mr. Budd, and there was a faraway look in his eyes, as though he was thinking deeply.

'What about Snodland? You're not going to say that he's the mysterious Jackson you've been talking about?'

'No, I'm not goin' to say that, Walton, though he may well be for all I know. What I *am* goin' ter say is that Snodland's father died when he was four years old, an' his mother married again.'

'So what?' burst out Peter impatiently as the detective paused.

'She married again,' repeated Mr. Budd, and the lids had dropped so low over his eyes that he looked as if he were on the point of falling asleep. 'She married a feller called Marie.'

'Everitt Marie?' exclaimed Peter.

'No — not Everitt Marie,' murmured the detective, shaking his head. 'Everitt Marie's father.'

'So Snodland is . . . ' began the reporter.

'Everitt Marie's half-brother,' broke in Mr. Budd. 'All very interestin' an' peculiar, ain't it?'

28

Major Snodland Makes a Statement

'Interesting, certainly,' said Peter, looking a little puzzled, 'but why peculiar?'

'You'd be surprised,' said Mr. Budd evasively. '*I* think it's peculiar.'

Mr. Budd had said all he intended to say on the subject, and refused to discuss it further, to Peter's intense exasperation. Boyder returned at that moment with the information that he had arranged for the men to watch the ruins. They were on their way from Barnford with full instructions.

'Come along up to my room,' said Mr. Budd. 'I've got somethin' I want to discuss with you. I'll see you later, Walton,' he added as they left the coffee-room, and Peter was forced to accept this dismissal with as much good grace as possible.

When he had shut the door and

ensconced Boyder in a chair, the detective produced the report he had received from Scotland Yard and acquainted the local man with its contents. Boyder was surprised and interested.

'It certainly looks as though your idea was right,' he remarked thoughtfully. 'Do you think this man Snodland is the one we're after?'

'I wouldn't go so far as to say that,' said Mr. Budd cautiously. 'When Marie was dyin' in prison, he sent for somebody called Jackson to tell 'im, in my opinion, about the Abbot's Key containin' the secret of the treasure. Now the most likely person 'ud be a relative, wouldn't it?'

'His half-brother, Snodland.' Boyder nodded. 'Snodland said he'd heard of Marie, but never met him.'

'Naturally he wouldn't want us to know of any connection. If he's the feller at the bottom of all this business, an' after them statues, he'd want to try an' block all trails that might put us wise. He bought Marie's dog, Bisto, an' he wasn't livin' here then, so unless he knew more about Marie than he admitted, how would he have known about the dog? If he isn't Jackson, I'll bet he could give a pretty good guess who is. S'pose we go along an' see him an' try an' make him talk?'

'Mightn't it put him on his guard?'

'If he's Jackson, he'll be on his guard already, an' if he isn't, then we may as well find out how he fits into the scheme of things.'

'All right,' agreed Boyder. 'I shall be mighty glad when this business is settled. The chief constable is getting touchy about it. This is something big and he wants to shine. It's understandable in a way, I suppose.'

'He can shine as much as he likes,' grunted Mr. Budd as they went down the stairs, 'so long as he don't interfere an' spoil things.'

* * *

Major Snodland was in when they arrived at Abbot's Rest. Mrs. Blimber, a thin woman who looked as if she had a perpetual cold in the head, and who was energetically cleaning the hall, admitted

316

them and ushered them into the sitting-room where Snodland was reading a newspaper.

'Back again?' he said when the curious charwoman had reluctantly gone and closed the door. 'What is it this time?'

'In a way it's the same thing,' said Mr. Budd. 'Certain information has come into our possession which we should like to discuss with you.'

'Go ahead,' said Snodland, getting up.

'I'm given to understand,' said Mr. Budd, 'that your father, Francis Snodland, died when you were only three years old an' that your mother married again, is that right?'

A flicker of uneasiness appeared in the protruding eyes, and Snodland gave a slight nod.

'She married a man named Halford Marie,' went on Mr. Budd, 'an' they had a son they named Everitt. The same feller who was arrested for fraud an' died in Wormwood Scrubbs prison.'

'Well, what about it?' snapped Major Snodland. 'What concern is all this of yours?'

'You an' Everitt Marie were half-brothers,' said the detective. 'We've reason to believe that Everitt Marie, although he's been dead for several months, is very closely connected with these two murders. We believe that Marie was in possession of a secret when he died, an' we believe that this secret is indirectly connected with the motive for the murder of Lloyd Gibbs an' Rita Claydon.'

Major Snodland licked his suddenly dry lips and his eyes strayed to the sideboard, rested for a moment on the bottle of whisky that stood there, and flickered uneasily back to Mr. Budd. 'To — to what secret do you refer?' he asked with a slight stammer.

'I think you know, Major Snodland,' murmured Mr. Budd softly. 'I'm pretty sure you've heard of the Twelve Apostles.'

'You mean the supposed hidden treasure of Felsbank Abbey? Yes, of course I've heard of it. Everybody in Monk's Ferry has heard of it.'

'But not quite in the way you have. You know that Everitt Marie had stumbled on

318

the secret of where these twelve silver statues are hidden, don't you?'

'I haven't the least idea what you're talking about. If, as you say, Marie knew the hiding-place of this treasure, I wasn't aware of it.'

'You never heard of the Abbot's Key, I suppose?'

'No, never.'

Mr. Budd sighed wearily. 'Or a feller by the name o' Jackson?' he went on.

'No,' Snodland answered. 'I should like to know where all this is leading.'

'I'm afraid it's leadin' to trouble,' murmured the superintendent, shaking his head sadly. 'An' it'll be your trouble.'

'Is that a threat?' demanded Snodland quickly.

'A threat?' Mr. Budd's gaze was blandly innocent. 'Dear me, no. It's just a friendly warnin'. Why did Mrs. Rita Claydon attend Marie's trial?'

'Did she?'

'Yes, Major Snodland, she did. I saw her there myself. It's a queer thing, too, that your friend, Withers, was at Wormwood Scrubbs when Marie died.'

'Why is it queer?' asked the ginger-haired man, and once more his eyes went longingly to the sideboard and the whisky bottle. 'I suppose there were a great many other people there, too.'

'Everythin' comes back to Everitt Marie, don't it? You, Mrs. Claydon, an' Spooky Withers — an', of course, this feller Jackson who he sent for before he died. You might call Marie the cause, an' all you people bein' here together, the effect. It's very funny.'

'It doesn't strike me as being particularly humorous,' snapped Snodland. 'I personally knew very little about Marie. I'll admit that he was my half-brother, but we had little in common.'

'He made you an allowance of a thousand pounds a year while he was in a position to do it. There seems ter be a lot in common about that to me.'

Major Snodland's red face slowly turned purple, and his eyes glinted viciously. 'How did you know that?' he demanded harshly.

'I know quite a lot o' things,' replied Mr. Budd, yawning. 'That's quite a tidy sum — particularly when you don't get it anymore. They tell me them silver statues are worth a million quid — that 'ud be pretty good compensation for the loss of a thousand a year.'

'May I ask what you're insinuating?'

'I'm insinuatin' that you an' Withers an' this woman Claydon were after that million quid. I'm insinuatin' that you *knew* Marie held the secret, an' you were after it. An' I'm insinuatin' that it would be better if you came clean instead of lyin' an' hidin' up, an' that if you don't you'll very likely find yourself detained on suspicion of knowin' more about these murders than you appear, an' Withers with you.'

Major Snodland gulped noisily. The rage died from his eyes and fear took its place. He passed the tip of his tongue over his lips, strode to the sideboard and poured himself a drink, which he drank quickly. 'Supposing . . . supposing we *were* after the treasure?' he said hesitantly. 'What about it? There's nothing illegal in it.'

Mr. Budd had sized up his man pretty

well, he thought. Major Snodland was no fighter. At the first hint of danger, his bluster collapsed like a pricked balloon. 'That depends on the methods used,' he said. 'Murder's illegal, an' so is abduction.'

'I had nothing to do with that,' declared Snodland, now thoroughly alarmed. 'I swear I had nothing — '

'You can tell that to the lawyer who prepares your defence,' said Mr. Budd. 'Maybe the jury 'ull believe yer an' maybe they won't.'

'But you can't arrest me for something I know nothing about!' exclaimed Snodland, his face twitching nervously. 'Anyway, the whole thing wasn't *my* idea. It was Rita's and Withers's — ' He checked himself quickly, but Mr. Budd pounced on the last part of his remark.

'Oh, it was Mrs. Claydon's an' Spooky Withers's idea, was it?' he said softly. 'An' what *was* this idea? The murder of Lloyd Gibbs?'

'No, no,' interrupted Snodland hastily. 'I had nothing to do with that. All we were interested in was the treasure.'

'How did you come to know that Marie held the secret?' demanded Mr. Budd. 'Did he tell you?'

'Withers told me,' answered Snodland. 'It was Withers who suggested the whole thing to Rita. You see — '

'Just one minute,' broke in the detective. 'We'll 'ave this in order, if you don't mind. You wish to make a statement?'

Major Snodland hesitated, met Mr. Budd's stern and suddenly very wide-awake eyes, and nodded. 'Yes,' he said reluctantly. 'I'll make a statement.'

'Then we'll take it down in writin' an' you can sign it,' said Mr. Budd with great affability. 'Superintendent Boyder here can witness it, an' everythin' will be right and proper. Maybe you've got some paper we could use?'

Snodland went over to a desk in the corner and produced a writing-block. With ill grace he thrust it into the detective's hand.

'Thank you,' said Mr. Budd. He sat down at the table, laid the writing-block in front of him, and unscrewed the cap of his fountain-pen. 'Now,' he said, looking up, 'I'm ready to hear what you've got ter say.'

29

The Abbot's Key

'How shall I begin?' Snodland asked nervously.

'Well,' said Mr. Budd, staring sleepily at the ceiling, 'what's your full name?'

'Anthony Snodland.'

'I, Anthony Snodland, havin' been warned that it may be used in evidence, make this statement of my own free will an' without any coercion whatsoever.'

'Is all that necessary?'

'Well, it makes it all legal an' above-board. I'll just get that down an' then you can go on.'

While he was getting it down, Major Snodland helped himself to another drink. And then he began, hesitantly and with many pauses and corrections, a long and rather rambling statement which, shorn of all its trimmings, amounted to this:

He had never really been on intimate terms with his half-brother, but Marie had apparently considered it his duty to look after Snodland when he himself had become a rich man. He had made him an allowance of a thousand pounds a year and had later bought Abbot's Rest and given it to him. When the crash came and Marie was arrested, the allowance ceased. Snodland had saved a certain amount of money, but it wasn't a lot and he was getting worried about the future. He had no trade, and so far as his rank of major went, it had only been a temporary one during the war of 1914–18 and did not carry a pension. He was getting seriously alarmed about his future financial position when he received a letter from Rita Claydon, who had been an intimate friend of Marie's for some time — it was Snodland's opinion that she had been something more than a friend, but if this was the case, Marie and she had been so discreet that nobody was aware of it. In fact, very few people knew that she and Marie were even friends. Marie had been like that. He loved to be mysterious.

When he was only twenty-one, he had suddenly got married, and nobody, not even his own mother, had known anything about it until he announced that he was divorced eighteen months later.

Rita Claydon had written to Snodland, asking if he would meet her in London. The letter had come three days before the murder of Gibbs, and he had gone to keep the appointment wondering what she wanted. He had only met her once before with Marie, and he was curious to know why she had written to him. He quickly found out.

Without beating about the bush, she told him that it had come to her knowledge that Marie had discovered where the treasure of Felsbank Abbey had been hidden. It was worth a considerable sum, and she wanted to know if he would help her get it. This was the first he knew anything about Marie having discovered the secret. He had asked for more particulars before committing himself, and she had told him that a man called Withers, who had been in Wormwood Scrubbs when Marie died, had overheard him telling a man named Jackson about the treasure. The secret was concealed in the Abbot's Key at a house called Abbotsway. Withers had been on orderly duty in the prison infirmary at the time, which had given him the chance to listen. Marie had once mentioned Rita Claydon to him, and as soon as he was released from prison himself, Withers had come to her and suggested that they should go after the treasure themselves. She immediately remembered that Snodland lived in the district, and had thought that his cottage would make a good place from which to work. Was he interested?

Snodland was definitely interested. He suggested that they should both come down and stay at Abbot's Rest and discuss the matter further, and they did so. The difficulty they had to overcome was finding the Abbot's Key. Abbotsway was occupied. Even if they had known where Marie had put the key, it was going to be a difficult job to find. Rita suggested that Withers, who knew more about faking ghosts than anybody, should try and frighten the Shannons away. There was already a wave of superstition in the village, and she thought it wouldn't be difficult. They started to lay their plans, and then had come the news of Eileen Shannon's abduction and the sudden evacuation of the Shannon family. What they had been trying to achieve had been achieved for them.

Withers had wanted to go and break into Abbotsway that night, but Rita wouldn't hear of it. She would go herself and spy out the ground. She had done so, and the next they heard that she had been killed, like Lloyd Gibbs, in the abbey ruins. That, in brief, was all Major Snodland knew.

Mr. Budd read the statement aloud, and Snodland signed it, the detective and Superintendent Boyder appending their signatures as witnesses.

'Well,' said Mr. Budd, folding up the sheets carefully and putting them in his pocket, 'that's that. It's cleared the air a bit, but not very much. You've no idea who this man Jackson is?'

Major Snodland set down the glass he had just emptied and shook his head. 'No.

Rita wondered that, too. He must have been somebody Marie was pretty closely tied up with, or he wouldn't have sent for him when he knew he was dying.'

'Withers heard the whole interview?' murmured the detective. 'Maybe he could help. Where is he?'

'He went down to the village for something. He ought to have been back by now.'

Mr. Budd thoughtfully caressed his chin. 'You've no idea whereabouts at Abbotsway this key is ter be found?' he asked after a pause.

Snodland shook his head. 'No. If we'd known that, it would've been much easier. Marie may have told Jackson. Withers couldn't hear some of what he said, his voice was so weak. All he was able to hear was about the treasure and that the secret was in a key Marie had found, which was at Abbotsway. According to Withers he was very weak, and his speech was difficult and disjointed.'

'I'll have to have a word with him,' said Mr. Budd. 'Maybe he can remember something that'll help us to find this feller

330

Jackson. You said that Marie was married when he was twenty-one. Who did he marry?'

'A woman named Bentham,' answered Snodland a little wearily. 'She was older than he was. A pretty bad lot from what I know, which isn't much. She was mixed up with a whole string of other men, and — '

'Was there any family?' asked Mr. Budd suddenly. 'I mean, was there a child from the marriage?'

'I never heard of one, but there might have been. Marie was so confoundedly secretive about things that nobody would have known.'

'An' he divorced this woman eighteen months after they was married?' said Mr. Budd, wrinkling his brows. 'Hm. If there *had* been a child, Marie would probably have got the custody of it.'

'Are you suggesting that this child might be Jackson?'

'I was thinking something of the sort,' admitted Mr. Budd. He rose to his feet, went over to the window and looked out. 'Can we borrow your dog?' he asked, turning suddenly.

Major Snodland gaped in astonishment. 'Bisto? What the devil for?'

'Never mind what for,' said the detective impatiently. 'Can we have him for an hour or so?'

'I suppose you can. You'll have to put him on a leash. He won't go with you otherwise.'

'That's all right. Get him, will you?'

Major Snodland, the picture of bewilderment, went in search of the bull terrier. Boyder, equally amazed, looked at his confrere with raised eyebrows. 'What in the world are you going to do with the dog?' he asked.

'That dog found the Abbot's Key once,' Mr. Budd said in a low voice. 'I'm goin' ter see if he can find it again.'

'You mean — '

'Shhh.' Mr. Budd made a warning gesture as Snodland came back with the dog on a leash. Bisto was plainly delighted at the prospect of a walk and wagged his stumpy tail in joyous anticipation.

'Here you are,' said Snodland, handing

the leash to the detective. 'Look after him, won't you? I'm rather fond of that dog.'

Bisto, his ears cocked alertly, looked up at Mr. Budd and then at his master. He appeared a little puzzled, but he trotted to the door with the detective, although he kept looking back to see if Snodland were coming too.

'Go on . . . good dog,' said his master, and Bisto, deciding that in spite of the unusualness of the proceedings everything must be all right, allowed Mr. Budd to lead him out the front door and down the path to the road. Here he seemed to be a little uncertain as to whether he would go any further. He held back reluctantly, looking up at Mr. Budd and then back at the gate. The detective coaxed him along, however, and got him as far as the Abbotsway road. When he arrived at this point, the dog's mental attitude underwent a sudden change. Instead of hanging back, he suddenly darted forward, dragging on the lead with such eagerness that Mr. Budd had to increase his pace to keep up with him.

'When we get a little bit further on,' panted Mr. Budd breathlessly, 'we'll leave the road an' take ter the wood. We can reach the back of the house that way without advertisin' ourselves.'

Bisto was quite willing to plunge into the woods. He was enjoying himself hugely and no longer seemed to have any misgivings. He scampered along with great glee, his muzzle almost touching the ground and his tail bristling with excitement. And as they neared Abbotsway, his delight and excitement increased until he broke into joyful whimpering.

'He remembers his old home,' said Mr. Budd. 'I expect he's got an idea that he's goin' ter see Marie.'

They came to the back gate at last and slipped through into the garden. Bisto sniffed the air with eager delight and strained on the leash as they made their way towards the house. Once more Mr. Budd negotiated the small window at the rear, then Boyder lifted the dog through and got in himself.

Bisto could scarcely contain himself as Mr. Budd slipped off the lead and let him free. He ran about, nosing in corners and circling round in a paroxysm of joy, and then went scampering through into the great hall. Here he stopped and stared at the staircase, his ears cocked alertly. Then he went bounding up, and when they followed they found him scratching at a closed door.

'Shannon's study,' remarked Mr. Budd, 'an' most likely Marie's too.' He opened the door and Bisto rushed in with a sharp, welcoming bark. But when he saw that the room was empty, he stopped dead and looked back at Boyder and Mr. Budd, the picture of perplexed disappointment.

'He expected to find 'is old master,' murmured Mr. Budd. 'He prob'ly spent a lot o' time up here with Marie.'

The dog was nosing and sniffing round the room. He trotted to the chair behind the desk and stood up on his hind legs, looking at its emptiness in disappointed wonder. With one fore-paw still on the seat, he looked questioningly at Mr. Budd and Boyder. He was asking, quite clearly, why the chair was unoccupied.

Standing silently beside the local man, Mr. Budd watched him. Would his experiment prove a fiasco, or would Bisto be able to lead them to the Abbot's Key? It was a forlorn hope — an idea that had occurred to him on the spur of the moment.

Bisto left the empty chair reluctantly and stood looking at them with every evidence of dejection.

'Find, old chap,' said Mr. Budd encouragingly. 'Go on, seek it out — *find it!*'

The dog pricked up his ears, whimpered, and began to run about the room, sniffing in the corners.

'It's a million to one against his finding the key,' said Boyder. 'It may be anywhere in the house.'

'It was just a possibility. I thought he might nose it out. If this was Marie's study, it's the most likely place, an' if the dog happened ter be with him when he hid the — '

'Look,' broke in Boyder. 'What's he doing at the fireplace?'

The dog had stopped and was sniffing eagerly at the hearth. Presently he began to scratch at the old bricks, uttering little excited cries and pausing to look round appealingly.

'Maybe we're goin' to be lucky after all,' said Mr. Budd, and he went over to the dog.

'What is it, old chap? Find it then!'

Bisto gave a sharp bark and redoubled his scratching. The detective stooped and peered at the place he was so interested in. The hearth, like all the hearths at Abbotsway, was paved with old time-mellowed red bricks. The spot where Bisto was scratching so energetically was exactly like the rest, except that the cement round one brick looked a trifle fresher than the rest.

'I think we are in luck,' murmured Mr. Budd. 'Go an' see if you can find somethin' we can loosen this cement with.'

Boyder went away and, after a long interval, came back with a coke hammer and a screwdriver. 'Will these do?' he asked.

Mr. Budd nodded. 'Just hold the dog back,' he said, and Boyder gripped Bisto by the collar and dragged him away, an operation which he resented strongly.

Kneeling down, the detective attacked the brick. After a little while he succeeded in loosening the cement round it, and, using the screwdriver as a lever, prised the brick up until he could lift it out with his fingers. Beneath it was a shallow cavity in which lay something wrapped in oilskin. Bisto went nearly wild with excitement, struggling to break away from Boyder's hold on his collar, as Mr. Budd lifted the object out and unwrapped it. It was a large rust-corroded key about six inches long.

'I think that's it,' the detective murmured. 'The Abbot's Key that so many people have been tryin' to find.'

30

'Jackson!'

Mr. Budd examined the key lying in the palm of his hand while Boyder peered over his shoulder and the dog Bisto leapt frantically round them. The key was very old and looked as though it had lain long in water, so crusted and eaten away was it by rust. There was nothing ornate about it. It was a heavy and solid piece of workmanship with simple wards. The only thing peculiar about it was that the end which protruded beyond the wards had been plugged with a cork — a new cork.

Mr. Budd removed the cork and squinted up the hollow barrel. There was something inside that looked like rolled paper. Taking a pin from the lapel of his coat, which he invariably kept there ready for the buttonhole he always wore when he was at home and had access to his garden, he carefully teased the paper out of the key.

It proved to be a strip of ancient stained parchment. When he unrolled it, he saw that it contained several lines of crabbed writing in ink that had faded to a faint brown. But he could make nothing of it, for it was written in Latin. He sniffed disgustedly and looked at Boyder. 'Well, here's the secret of the Twelve Apostles,' he remarked. 'But it's double Dutch ter me.'

'We'll have to get it translated,' said Boyder. 'So *that's* behind all these strange doings.'

Mr. Budd nodded. 'That's it,' he said gently. 'An' now all we've got ter do is to find this feller, Jackson.'

'You've found him,' said a muffled voice huskily. 'Keep still or you'll get hurt.'

Mr. Budd swung round. In the open doorway stood a figure. It was clad in a long grey habit with a cowl that covered the head. The face beneath was concealed behind a dark handkerchief, and in one gloved hand was an automatic pistol.

340

'Who are you?' demanded the detective.

'I'm Jackson,' said the man in the doorway. 'I want that key. If you're wise you'll give it to me.'

Mr. Budd was silent. He was looking at Bisto. The dog was staring at the man in the doorway and his stumpy tail was wagging furiously.

'Come on,' went on the unknown impatiently. 'I can't wait all day. Hand over the key.'

'You can't get away with this,' said Boyder sternly. 'Put that pistol down.'

'Shut up and do as I say,' snapped the man in the doorway, 'or I warn you it'll be the worse for you. I'm serious. I want that key and I mean to have it.'

'Take it, then!' snarled Mr. Budd, and unexpectedly flung the heavy key full at him. It struck the man in the face and he uttered a cry of pain and staggered. At the same moment, Bisto, with a delighted bark, sprang forward and made a snap at the key where it had fallen to the floor. He became entangled with the unknown's legs and the man overbalanced, grasping wildly at the doorframe to save himself from falling.

Boyder saw his chance and took it. Leaping forward, he grasped the man's wrist, jerked the pistol from his hand, and thrusting out his foot, tripped him neatly. He fell heavily, and Mr. Budd, coming over, calmly sat on him.

'Now,' he said triumphantly, 'let's have a look at you, Mr. Jackson.' He pulled back the cowl and with his other hand wrenched down the dark handkerchief that covered his face.

It was Spooky Withers!

'Well, well,' murmured Mr. Budd. 'Now fancy that. So you're Jackson, are you? Who'd have believed it?'

'Get up,' grunted Withers, glaring at him. 'Get up, will you? You're crushing my breastbone.'

'Never mind yer breastbone. I don't weigh more'n eighteen stone, an' that won't 'urt you. What d'yer mean by sayin' you're Jackson?'

Spooky Withers looked at him spitefully. 'It was as good a name as any other,' he answered, 'and if I'd got away with that key you'd have thought it *was* Jackson.'

'I see,' said Mr. Budd. 'I s'pose this thing was part of the outfit for playin' ghosts an' frightenin' away the Shannons?' He fingered the grey habit.

'I don't know what you're talking about,' muttered Withers.

'It's no good pretendin',' said Mr. Budd, shaking his head. 'Your friend Major Snodland's told us all about it, an' what's more I've got it all down in writin' an' signed.'

'Snodland's told you? Why, the white-livered . . .' Withers broke into a string of unprintable expletives concerning Major Snodland's origin, his life, death, and ultimate destination.

'Hush,' said Mr. Budd in awed admiration. 'You'll shock all yer spirit friends! Now, how did you get here?'

'I walked,' snarled Withers. 'Will you get up off my chest?'

'If you're goin' ter be sensible,' said the detective, and he hoisted himself to his feet with difficulty. 'I s'pose you came here, knowin' the place was empty, to have a look for this key on your own account?'

Withers got up with as much dignity as he could muster. 'You can suppose what you like,' he said ungraciously.

'It's not quite as easy as that, you know,' put in Boyder sternly. 'You can be charged with being found on unoccupied premises with intent to commit a felony, and with unlawfully being in possession of a firearm.'

'Couldn't you drag in arson, forgery, dope-peddling, and a few other charges?' grunted Spooky Withers.

'We might drag in murder, unless you're very careful,' snapped Mr. Budd. 'I'd advise you ter keep a civil tongue in your 'ead unless you want ter find yerself in serious trouble.'

Mr. Withers looked at him and apparently came to the conclusion that discretion was the better part of valour, for his belligerent attitude became distinctly modified. 'I was only joking,' he said.

'That's all right,' answered Mr. Budd heartily. 'We've all had a good laugh an' the joke's over. Now we'll get down to serious business. You was a hospital orderly when this feller Jackson visited Marie, an' you saw him. What was he like?'

'A very ordinary-looking man. I don't suppose I'd recognize him again if I saw him. It was a very wet day, and he was muffled up in a coat and wore a wide-brimmed hat pulled down over his eyes. He gave me the impression of being young — round about twenty-six to thirty, I should say. I might recognize his voice if I heard it. I've a good memory for voices, better than I have for faces.'

'Listen,' interrupted Boyder suddenly. 'There's somebody in the house below.'

Bisto, who had been calmly lying down trying to gnaw pieces out of the Abbot's Key, rose up on his haunches and growled. Mr. Budd heard a soft step in the hall and went quickly and silently to the door.

'Who's there?' he called sharply.

'Only me,' answered the voice of Peter Walton. 'What's the idea? Do you live here now?'

345

Mr. Budd heard a quick breath behind him and, looking round, caught sight of Spooky Withers's face. It was a mixture of surprise, doubt, and — recognition!

'That's it,' he whispered. 'That voice! *That is the voice of Jackson!*'

Although he had been expecting the answer, Mr. Budd experienced something that was akin to a physical shock. Peter Walton! Yet *was* it so impossible? Walton and Lloyd Gibbs had been friends . . . Walton had tried to account for Gibbs's presence in Monk's Ferry by saying that he had come to see a woman, and there had been no evidence to bear out this statement . . . Walton had tried to throw suspicion on to Michael Shannon . . . A hundred and one things shook up in Mr. Budd's mind and dropped into place. Something of the shock he had experienced was repeated in the face of Boyder.

'Are you sure?' whispered the local man.

Spooky Withers nodded. 'Quite sure,' he answered. 'I'd be willing to swear to it.'

'Shhh,' murmured Mr. Budd. 'He's coming up.'

Peter Walton's footsteps came quickly up the stairs, and a second later he appeared in the open doorway, the usual grin on his freckled face. 'Hello, hello!' he greeted breezily. 'What's going on?' He caught sight of the dishevelled and strangely garbed Mr. Withers and his eyebrows shot upwards. 'Good Lord,' he exclaimed, 'have you caught the ghost?'

'Yes, we've caught him, Walton,' said Mr. Budd gravely. 'D'you recognize him?'

'Recognize him? No. How should I? I've never seen him before.' The reporter looked at Mr. Withers blankly.

'Are you certain of that? Didn't you see him when you visited Everitt Marie in Wormwood Scrubbs?'

'I don't know what you mean.' The blank expression remained on Peter Walton's face. 'I never visited Marie in Wormwood Scrubbs.'

'That's a lie!' broke in Spooky Withers harshly. 'You came to see him when he was dying. You were the man called Jackson to whom he confided the secret of the Abbot's Key and the Twelve Apostles.'

'I think you must be mad,' exclaimed Peter Walton, looking in bewilderment from one to the other. 'You don't believe all this nonsense, do you, Budd?'

It was a superb piece of acting, and even Mr. Budd was almost taken in. And then, in trying to consolidate the impression he had created, Peter Walton made a slip. 'It's fantastic,' he went on. 'How can this man presume to identify somebody he only saw for a few seconds?' He realized his mistake the moment he had made it, but it was too late to rectify.

'How do *you* know that?' snapped Mr. Budd. 'How do *you* know that he only saw this man Jackson for only a few seconds? You couldn't know that unless you was there.'

Peter's eyes narrowed, and in some queer, subtle way the whole of his face seemed to change. The impudent, rather boyish expression faded and was replaced by a crafty, hard, cruel look, as though some invisible hand had snatched away a mask. He looked quickly from one to the other, and then, before they realized what he was going to do, he caught the door handle, pulled the door shut with a bang, and turned the key in the lock.

They heard his retreating footsteps go thudding down the stairs as Mr. Budd leapt to the door and shook the handle. But the door was of solid oak and fitted tightly. It refused to budge in spite of all his efforts and the efforts of Boyder, who tried to help him.

'It looks as though we're goin' to lose him after all,' panted the detective. 'By the time we get that door open, he'll be well away.'

He went over to the window, pushed upon the casement, and looked out. He could see across the garden to the main gate and the ruins of the abbey, but there was no sign of Peter Walton. He must have left by the back gate and taken to the woods. Taking a deep breath, Mr. Budd shouted. His voice echoed back from the trees, but nobody answered.

He shouted again, hoping that Boyder's men would have reached the ruins and would hear him. But there was no reply, and he had opened his mouth for the third time when a man carrying a hoe came quickly round the corner of the house and looked up. It was the gardener.

'Wot are you makin' all that row about?' he demanded truculently. 'Who are yer, an wot's going on 'ere?'

'I'm Superintendent Budd. We're locked in. Come and open the door.'

'Locked in, are yer? Wot about that feller who came dartin' out just now? Was 'e with you?'

'He locked us in,' said Mr. Budd. 'Which way did he go? He's the man who killed Gibbs.'

''E didn't go anywhere,' said the gardener with great satisfaction. 'I thought it was queer, 'im runnin' away like that, with the 'ouse empty.'

'What d'you mean, 'e didn't go anywhere?'

'I slugged 'im one with the 'andle o' me 'oe. It don't look as though 'e'll come round fer another ten minutes or so!'

31

The Twelve Apostles

After two busy weeks, during which he had worked almost unceasingly to prepare his case against Peter Walton, Mr. Budd, looking more weary and sleepy-eyed than usual, sat one morning in the office of the assistant commissioner at Scotland Yard, and made his final verbal report to the interested Colonel Blair.

'I think it's all pretty clear now, sir,' he said with the complacent satisfaction of a man who has completed a difficult job and done it well. 'This feller Walton was Everitt Marie's son by 'is first marriage, an' he's always been a pretty bad lot from all accounts. He was in trouble with the police at eighteen and again at twenty — both times on a charge of stealin'. After the last occasion he changed his name to Jackson, an' under that alias he appears to have got mixed up with some of the worst characters in London. Marie had apparently washed his hands of him, makin' him a small allowance on the condition that he kept out of his way. His knowledge of crime an' criminals, which he got at first hand under the name o' Jackson, enabled him to make a bit of extra money writin' articles for various newspapers under the name o' Peter Walton, an' eventually to get a job as a reporter with the *Post-Courier*. Quite a lot o' the crimes he reported were instigated by himself under the name of Jackson. He was at this time livin' two distinct an' separate lives, one as Jackson in a small flat at Brixton — the address that Marie knew, an' where he used to send the allowance — an' the other as Peter Walton, in a flat in Gray's Inn Road. He was so clever at handlin' these two identities that no one seems ter 'ave suspected him. At least, not for some time; an' then Lloyd Gibbs, with whom Walton got friendly, began to have his suspicions.

'These culminated round about the time o' Marie's death. Marie, when he knew that he was dyin', seems to have forgiven his son fer all his misdeeds. Anyhow, we know that he sent fer him an' told him of the existence of the Twelve Apostles an' that the secret of where they was hid was to be found in the Abbot's Key which he'd hidden under a brick in the study at Abbotsway before his arrest.

'The prospect of a million quid ter be picked up with very little trouble filled Walton, or Jackson, whichever yer like to call 'im, with a determination to get it. The first step was to get hold of the Abbot's Key, for without that he didn't know where these statues were from Adam. But Abbotsway was occupied. So he sought out a little burglar called Lew Cator, explained what he was after, and offered Cator a share of the treasure if he'd break into Abbotsway an' get the key.

'But Lew refused. He wasn't a bad little feller as crooks go, an' he didn't much like Jackson. He had a reputation for violence, an' Lew hated violence in any form. By refusin', he signed his death warrant; for Jackson, afraid that he might talk, ran him down in a car one dark night an' injured him so badly that he died.

'In the meanwhile, Gibbs had been quietly substantiatin' his suspicions against Walton. He had discovered his alias of Jackson, an' quite a lot of other things that would have got him a heavy sentence if he chose to open his mouth. He had also found out his connection with Cator, and guessed that his death hadn't been an accident. He taxed Walton with what he knew an' Walton got the wind up. Gibbs knew too much — a great deal too much. If he liked to open his mouth, he could send Walton to the trap. In fact, he threatened to do so.

'To keep him quiet, Walton told him the story of the Twelve Apostles an' offered to share the treasure with him in return for his silence. Gibbs, who, although he made a lot of money, was always in debt, fell for the possibility o' gettin' hold of such a large sum, an' agreed to keep his mouth shut an' to help. He went down to Monk's Ferry to try an' find out how it would be possible to get hold of the Abbot's Key. It was for this reason that he scraped up an acquaintance with Michael Shannon. Durin' his stay in Monk's Ferry an' his exploration of the ruins — I think he had some idea of tryin' ter find the treasure for himself an' double-crossin' Walton — he stumbled on the secret entrance to the underground vaults, which he showed Walton. An' that was how he came by his death.

'Walton, chafing under the bonds that Gibbs drew tighter at every meetin', decided to rid himself of this feller who knew so much an' had it in his power to be so dangerous. He waited for him one night, when they had arranged to meet, an' as he appeared, stabbed him — an' that was the end of Gibbs bein' a danger.'

Mr. Budd paused and moistened his lips. He was a little dry from so much talking. Colonel Blair poured out a glass of water and pushed it across the desk.

'Thank you, sir,' murmured the superintendent, and he sipped it gratefully. 'Well,' he continued, glancing at a notebook that lay open on his knee, 'I think you know most of the rest. Walton had brought a feller called Lisker an' installed him in the vaults under the ruins with a lot o' food an' odds an' ends. He was a poor half-witted feller who was so scared o' Walton — although he didn't know who he was — that he was completely under his thumb. Walton, with Lisker's help, carried out the abduction of Miss Shannon with the sole purpose of forcin' the Shannons to vacate the house so that he could get the Abbot's Key.' He stopped and took another sip of water.

'What about the murder of Rita Claydon?' asked the assistant commissioner. 'Why did he kill her?'

'That was done on the spur of the moment,' said Mr. Budd. 'She was on her way to Abbotsway to have a look round — she an' Snodland an' this feller Withers was after the Abbot's Key, too — when somethin' must have attracted her attention in the ruins. Maybe it was a light that wasn't visible to Sergeant Leek, who was followin' her, or somethin' like that. Anyway, she changed her mind an' reached the ruins just as Walton, in his monk's disguise, was emergin' from the door in the tower. He had to kill her because she'd seen too much. He coshed Leek for the same reason, an' it's lucky fer him that it was no worse. I think he thought that Leek was with Claydon an' wanted ter find out how much they knew. When he did discover who Leek was, Lisker says he had some vague idea that he might be more useful alive. I think that's about all, sir.'

'Hm.' The assistant commissioner stared thoughtfully at his blotting-pad. 'An unusual business. You seem to have handled it very well, Superintendent.'

'Thank you, sir,' said the gratified Mr. Budd.

'There's one thing I can't understand,' went on Colonel Blair with a puzzled frown. 'How in the world did Walton — and these other people, for that matter — hope to move this treasure? A life-size statue in solid silver weighs a lot, and there are supposed to be twelve of them.'

'Well, sir,' remarked Mr. Budd, 'it 'ud depend quite a lot on *where* they was hid, wouldn't it? I don't think any of 'em had worked that out. They was waitin' to adapt an idea to circumstances. Walton thought of gettin' 'em one by one to the vaults under the old abbey, an' Snodland says that he an' Withers had decided to make the discovery public an' trust to the law of treasure trove.'

'Pretty clever idea of the old abbot's,' Colonel Blair murmured after a pause, 'to hide the statues in the vault in the churchyard. Nobody thought of looking for them there.'

'You'd never have thought they was anythin' but dead monks, sir,' said Mr. Budd.

'They'd cleared out the real coffins an' put 'em in that place under the abbey where you can see 'em now. When the old abbot had written out what he'd done with 'em, he put the parchment inside the key, plugged up the end, an' must have dropped it into the river Fell. I don't s'pose he ever thought the river 'ud dry up one day, or that a dog 'ud dig up the key centuries later.'

He finished the glass of water and wiped his lips. 'Monk's Ferry's full up o' professors and archaeologists and what-not,' he said with a chuckle. 'The village

358

shops an' the pub are doin' a roarin' trade.' He felt in his waistcoat pocket and produced one of his black cigars, caught the alarm in the assistant commissioner's eye, and regretfully put it back again. 'Miss Shannon's going to marry that feller Ashford,' he said. 'Colonel Shannon's a bit chastened since his trouble. I rather think his family 'ull find 'im a little more human in future.'

'There will only be his son left after the daughter's married, won't there?' said Colonel Blair.

'There'll only be himself an' Mrs. Shannon,' said Mr. Budd. 'You see, sir, Michael Shannon was secretly married ter that gal, Miss Gayling. That's what she was goin' ter tell me when she changed 'er mind. Nice gal — a very nice gal.' His hand strayed again unconsciously to his waistcoat pocket.

The assistant commissioner's eyes twinkled. 'Go and smoke one of those atrocious things,' he said with a wave of dismissal. 'Though how you can stand them beats me.'

'It's a matter o' use, sir,' said Mr.

Budd. He got up, lumbered to the door, and went out, closing it behind him. In the corridor he paused, took out a cigar, removed the band, lit it, and, trailing clouds of poisonous smoke behind him, made his way to his own office with an expression of the deepest content.

THE FACELESS ONES
GRIM DEATH
MURDER IN MANUSCRIPT
THE GLASS ARROW
THE THIRD KEY
THE ROYAL FLUSH MURDERS
THE SQUEALER
MR. WHIPPLE EXPLAINS
THE SEVEN CLUES
THE CHAINED MAN
THE HOUSE OF THE GOAT
THE FOOTBALL POOL MURDERS
THE HAND OF FEAR
THE SORCERER'S HOUSE
THE HANGMAN
THE CON MAN
MISTER BIG
THE JOCKEY
THE SILVER HORSESHOE
THE TUDOR GARDEN MYSTERY
THE SHOW MUST GO ON
SINISTER HOUSE
THE WITCHES' MOON
ALIAS THE GHOST
THE LADY OF DOOM

THE BLACK HUNCHBACK
PHANTOM HOLLOW
WHITE WIG
THE GHOST SQUAD
THE NEXT TO DIE
THE WHISPERING WOMAN

with Chris Verner:
THE BIG FELLOW

We do hope that you have enjoyed reading this large print book.

Did you know that all of our titles are available for purchase?

We publish a wide range of high quality large print books including:
Romances, Mysteries, Classics
General Fiction
Non Fiction and Westerns

Special interest titles available in large print are:
The Little Oxford Dictionary
Music Book, Song Book
Hymn Book, Service Book

Also available from us courtesy of Oxford University Press:
Young Readers' Dictionary
(large print edition)
Young Readers' Thesaurus
(large print edition)

For further information or a free brochure, please contact us at:
Ulverscroft Large Print Books Ltd.,
The Green, Bradgate Road, Anstey,
Leicester, LE7 7FU, England.
Tel: (00 44) **0116 236 4325**
Fax: (00 44) **0116 234 0205**

Other titles in the
Linford Mystery Library:

BLACK BARGAIN

Victor Rousseau

Joan Wentworth, a newly qualified nurse, nearly faints from the ether whilst assisting the famous surgeon, Dr. Lancaster, and is promptly suspended from her job. That evening, when she pleads with him to reinstate her, she is surprised to be invited to work at his hospice that serves the poor hill people of Pennsylvania. Joan accepts; but on her arrival at the remote institute, she finds herself plunged into an atmosphere of menace and mystery. No one there seems to be normal — not least Dr. Lancaster himself when he visits . . .

THE MYSTERY OF BLOODSTONE

V. J. Banis

Ancient Bloodstone Manor stands on a rocky knoll overlooking the village of Skull Point. What is the secret that sends Vanessa and her aged guardian, Tutrice, rushing there despite the violent raging of a storm? What keeps Vanessa's parents prisoner within its walls? Who is the mysterious sailor found half-drowned on the beach, wearing a bloodstone ring that Vanessa recognizes at once? Bloodstone — a house of secrets. A house of mystery. Mysteries that Vanessa must solve if she is ever to know happiness.

BLUE PERIL

Denis Hughes

Complicit in Doctor Brooking's efforts to create a monster, Gregory Conrad is ultimately forced to make the main contribution himself, losing his life in the process. However, Brooking discovers that the thing his genius has brought to life possesses a will of its own, as well as superhuman powers . . . Jerry Tern, an investigative reporter, and Vivienne Conrad, Gregory's sister, join forces to investigate her brother's disappearance, but soon become captives of the monster — the so-called Blue Peril of the popular press — and witness at first hand its reign of terror . . .

THE SECRET OF BENJAMIN SQUARE

Michael Kurland

When a stranger calls at their New England farmhouse to inform Nancy and her brother Robert that they are the heirs of a British nobleman, and that a fortune can be theirs if they agree to move to the ancestral home of Benjamin House in London, it seems like all their childhood dreams have come true. But upon arrival, Nancy is soon homesick — while Robert nearly loses his life in an 'accident'. Then there's the mysterious ancient riddle connected with the house that could point the way to hidden treasure . . .